The Efficient Life

LUTHER H. GULICK

In a merry mood   Laying down the law

Bending forward   In earnest argument

THE EXPRESSIONS OF VARIOUS EMOTIONS

An adverse proposition   Administering reproof

Attitude of urgent appeal   Pointing out fallacy

WITH THE MAINTENANCE OF A STRONG SPINE

The Efficient Life

By
LUTHER H. GULICK, M. D.

*Director of Physical Training
in the New York City Schools*

WITH DOUBLE-PAGE
FRONTISPIECE

New York
Doubleday, Page & Company
1907

I'HEODORE ROOSEVELT
WHO SOMETIMES LEADS THE SIMPLE LIFE,
WHO OFTEN LEADS THE STRENUOUS
LIFE, BUT WHO ALWAYS LEADS
THE EFFICIENT UFB
A WORD TO THE REAbM

Mj father once had medical care of an Hawsiiaii Chief, one of the Kamehamehas, I beliere. The treatment inrolved the use of a rather drastic pill crery evening for a number of days. The result of the first day's pill was so favourable that the chief took the rest of the boxful at once. His life was saved with great difficulty. So do not attempt to carry out all the suggestions in this book at once.

Take a chapter at a time. Mark freely all ideas that strike you favourably—jot down at the end of each chapter a few words to indicate the extent to which you think it applicable to yourself. Only undertake at first what seems to fit your one greatest need.

LUTHEB H. GULICK, M. D.

CONTENTS

ix

INTRODUCTION

"P\URING the past year one of my friends, a man of national reputation, died at the age of forty-six. It was said that his death was the result of overwork, and that the ultimate cause was failure of the kidneys. I knew his habits of work intimately, and I do not believe that the work alone could account for the sad result, which took him away in the prime of life and at a time when all his experiences qualified him to do better work than he had ever done before. I think the fundamental trouble was that he did not know how to run his physical machinery.

Shortly before this, another friend of mine, a man of international renown, died in his prime. Failure of the kidneys was also given as the immediate cause, and overwork as the predisposing cause. I have no doubt as to the correctness of this diagnosis; but I know that this man, although he was living a sedentary life, ate the quantity and kind of food of a man engaged in out-of-door, muscular work. Thus for many years he had seriously overtaxed his digestive organs, by overloading them with food. His heart was always rapid; his arteries became hard—^he had gout. Much, if not all of his trouble could probably have been removed had he consented to lessen his consumption of meat, thus decreasing the work required of the kidneys.

In the course of the past month one of the most brilliant young men of letters in America has been obliged to give up his work for a long period, in order to seek health. Another friend, a woman thirty-nine years of age, has for a great part of her life had violent headaches every week or ten days. She discovered two years ago that these were permanently cured by eating less starchy food. Her digestion of starch was imperfect. And so, I presume, all those who read this will be able to recall friends who have been either removed from life or from full service, at important and critical times, simply because they did not know how to conduct their lives.

This little book is entitled, "The Efficient Life," because efficiency is the ideal. To be strenuous is no end in itself. It is only when being strenuous is an aid to efficiency that it is worth while; and sometimes the quiet life is more effective than the strenuous one. The pursuit of health is not an end in itself. But to live a full, rich, efficient life is an end. I hope that these suggestions will prove in book form—as they have already proven in lecture form—useful in helping people to discover how they may improve that degree of efficiency which they individually possess.

Many of the chapters in this book were originally lectures delivered at the School of Pedagogy, New York University. A friend who had attended, took my notes, manuscript, and fragments, and wrote many of the chapters as they now stand. So if any of those who know me are so kind as to think that I have shown any new and unexpected gift of expression in this little volume, they must attribute it to Mr. Harry James Smith, who is at present one of the staff of the Atlantic Monthly,xvl Introduction

Thanks are due' the editors of The World's Work and of Good Housekeeping for permission to use articles which first appeared in those magazines.

Luther Halsey Gulick.

SPEED

CHAPTER I

TN RUNNING a short distance, such as fifty yards, one may put every ounce of his energy into each effort. Even breathing may be suspended to advantage, for the ribs when stationary give a firmer support to the muscles attached to them which are used in running. But the man who undertakes to run a mile at the pace of a fifty-yard dash will be badly beaten by the man who knows the pace of maximum efficiency and takes advantage of it.

The same law holds in intellectual undertakings. It is true that in times of emergency a man may work intensely and with profit, for eighteen hours per day: examinations may be passed, important addresses completed, or sudden and momentous cases at law prepared. In the interest of maximum efficiency one may subsist at such times upon small amounts of predigested foods, one may get along without exercise, without sleep, without relaxation of any kind. To a constitution well organised and intel-ligently controlled such spurts of work need not prove harmful. But the man who attempts to do the work of a year or of a lifetime at this pace will actually accomplish far less than if he went more slowly. It is not the point of maximum efficiency except for a spurt, and spurts do not win distance-races unless prepared for by a long period of wise running. The man who wins takes a pace that he can hold for the entire distance, and he will have a little extra "up his sleeve" to draw upon at the finish when the victory is a matter of a few feet or even of a few inches.

EFFICIENCY

CHAPTER II

TT IS the kind of work in which a man is engaged which determines for him the special meaning of the term efficiency. The success of his efforts may depend wholly upon the quantity of his output, or it may depend upon its quality. Quantity! Quality! Upon these two hang all the laws of efficiency.

Mere quantity is the measure of success for the man who shovels coal or digs in a ditch. Even the best of us have a considerable amount of pure hack-work to do: but as we go up the scale of human activity, quality counts more and more. The conditions of life when one can do work of the highest quality, demanding imagination, insight, vision, and creative power, are higher than the conditions when merely the maximum in quantity is demanded. The higher the quality of the work, the greater the nervous cost of it, and the more highly perfected must be the machine that does it.

The conditions for efficiency in the case 7

of the ordinary day labourer are not complex. His work is that of a coarse machine, turning out, like a grain thresher, a great amount of production relatively low in grade. His efficiency is but little disturbed by constant feeding upon indigestible victuals, by frequent carousals, by a dirty skin and bad air. Low-grade production does not need a high-grade organism.

But if under conditions of special stringency you press the day labourer to the utmost of his strength, one of two things happens. Either he goes to pieces and becomes useless; or his machinery alters, developing into something more highly organised, which requires more delicate care and which rebels more certainly under abuse. The conditions of health for him— that is to say, of "wholeness," of normal power—are more complex, more exacting. The coarser the machine, the more easily it maintains its balance. There is a criterion of efficiency for the threshing machine, but it is not that of a high-grade watch.

Men have in a few days developed ideas.formulated plans, written poems that were worth more to mankind than a lifetime of work whose value was estimated in terms of quantity. The health of the thinker, of the financier, of the executive genius, demands a momentary alertness of all the faculties, an ability to grasp, to originate, to carry out, a trained perception and an intelligent discrimination. He must be the master of a delicate, high-grade machine calculated to carry on high-grade work. His health is upon an absolutely different level from that of the farmhand or the coal shoveller.

Nothing could be more misleading than the familiar phrase, "healthy as a savage." The health of the savage is nothing to boast of. He has only a moderate control over his purely physical faculties. His power of endurance is limited, he is helpless in an emergency, he has no power of continued attention. Health such as his is a low-grade achievement.

For the larger number of city men and women, the conditions of efficiency are related more to the quality than to the quantity of their output. It pays for us to The Efficient Life learn how to run our machines on the higher levels of quality-efficiency. Live at your best," is a safe motto for everyone whose work calls for brain rather than brawn. The world rewards the man of brains. Through an excess of hack-work a man of native power may stand in the way of his own greatest success, for he is keeping his blood so full of the products of overwork and his nerve batteries so depleted that their best discharge is impossible. Big work demands high pressure, reserve power. Any engineer can pull his throttle wide open and soon lower the steam pressure to such an extent that great work is impossible till steam is raised again. People are constantly doing this. They do not keep up the supply of nervous energy to that point where big ideas or great execution are possible. They let themselves be so ground down by the deadly details of daily work that the real things, the great opportunities, slip by through lack of power to act at the critical moment.

To give one's self the best chance possible for insight, largeness of view, and inspiration, is clearly the part of wisdom. It may

Efficiency ll

be true, to be sure, that for a man who has never known any moments of larger life, who has never had any idea of value, the effort necessary to keep the machine on those high levels of power would not be worth while. A draught horse does not need for its kind of efficiency the same care that the race horse demands. The steam shovel does not need the special care bestowed upon a watch.

It is my conviction, however, that capabilities of a peculiar character exist in almost everyone; and that a man's value to society depends, to a large extent, upon his discovering and developing his special talent. The number of those who have a right to live complacently upon any other level than that of maximum efficiency is certainly small, for to do so implies that no further growth is possible for them.

It is not the intention in this book to provide an easy recipe for the development of genius. What it seeks is to enable each man to discover and secure for himself the best attainable conditions for his own daily life. It aims to apply to the various details of that life our present knowledge of physiology and psychology in a common sense and practical way.

For each of us it is possible to increase the duration of his best moments and to render them more frequent. It is also possible for us to reduce the number and the length of those periods of depression and low vitality when our work miscarries and our lives lack snap and enthusiasm. If we succeed in bringing about such a change, we shall have raised the whole plane of our living to something higher and more admirable. Our work will be productive of results that would otherwise have been quite beyond our reach.

There are conditions for each individual under which he can do the most and the best work. It is his business to ascertain those conditions and to comply with them.

LIFE THAT IS WORTH WHILE
CHAPTER III

T IFE is not only for work. It is for one's self and for one's friends. The degree of joy that a man finds in his work is due to two things: the intensity or fullness of his vitality, and the congenial character of the work itself. When one is thoroughly well and vigorous, the mere joy of living, of merely being alive, is very great. At such a time the nature of the work does not matter to a large extent. The sense of having power at your command, and the delight of exerting it even in coal shovelling or selling goods is enough. When one is full of life, the mere feel of fresh water or air on the skin, the taste of the plainest food, the exertion of muscular effort, the keeness of one's vision, the sight of colour in the sky, or the sound of the wind or the waves—it takes nothing beyond these to make one jubilant, enthusiastic.

To a man who is fatigued such sensations are sure to be without zest, even if they are not positively unpleasant. One of the com-

monest reasons for the blase or pessimistic feeUngs that so often come when youth is over is that one's system is constantly tired and rebels at additional sense-stimuli.

As a matter of fact, the vividness of one's feelings, of one's emotional experience, ought not to depart with youth. In a normal life it should deepen, to be sure, and be responsive to even larger and greater things; but it should retain its brightness and depth of colour. Love, hope, desire, appreciation, ambition and determination should grow, not diminish, with experience.

To live at a low level is to deaden every faculty for high thought and high feeling— it makes drudgery not only of work but also of life.

Many mothers slave for their children so many hours a day that they have but little energy left with which to enjoy them and love them. As a result, the dullness and drudgery of existence are all they come to experience. One mother of five children for years took at least an hour a day for rest and quiet reading alone by herself. Nothing but absolute necessity would

induce her to break into this hour. The result of this is not only that she has kept her own superb health, but more than this: she is a constant joy and inspiration to her children, her husband and her friends. It is true that she might have done more dusting or mending stockings than she actually accompHshed, but it would have been at the sacrifice of that whole part of her life which meant the most to herself and others. Instead of being able to enter upon the routine of each day with eagerness and satisfaction, it would have been the intolerable drudgery that it is for so many tired mothers. Even in the matter of the quantity of the work accomplished it seems probable that the daily rest was wise, for the remainder of the day was lived more intensely, its work was done more rapidly, and best of all, that balance and poise were preserved which we all lose if over tired. When fatigued to a certain point, every one of us loses his sense of proportion: we go on fretting over little things and doing ineffectual work just because we have not strength enough to stop.

Children inevitably grow away from mothers who do not keep themselves growing and their lives vivid. The mere ministering to the physical needs of children is not enough. They need our best selves after they are babies. During the years of their childhood and later we shall only serve them fully by living at our best, by living with inspiration and power. This it is impossible to do if we are daily over fatigued. We must live joyful, rich, vivid lives, not only for ourselves, but for our children and for all whom we love.

Full living, high-level living, is one of the conditions of continuous growth. Growth in power to see and to appreciate and to do should increase every year right into old age itself. You remember how the old scholar speaks in Browning's "By the Fireside":

My own, confirm me, if we tread

This pathway back, is it not in pride.

To think how little we dreamed it led To an age so blest that by its side Youth seems the waste indeed ?

It is certain that if a man, who starts out with a good heredity, sets himself at the

eflFort of constantly living at his best, the right kind of growth will come to him. If we take the machine at any stage and crowd it to its full capacity every day, we not only get low-level work from it, but there is failure all along the line. We bless the world by being happy, full of dash and vim, ready for any enterprise, alert for the new idea or the new application of the old one.

For a man to look back at childhood as the one happy time in life shows that he has missed something important. The happiest people are the men and women in the full maturity of their powers, who have kept youth's vividness of feeling, but who have added to this those great resources of life that are not open to children.

This matter of keeping one's self on a high level relates then not only to better work, but in an equally important degree to the attainment of a fuller, richer, more joyous life.

STATES OF MIND AND STATES OF BODY

CHAPTER IV

PSYCHOLOGISTS are learning nowa-days that it is impossible to treat the mind and the body as if they were really distinct. They have discovered that the two are so closely bound up together that nothing can affect one without affecting the other in a greater or less degree.

Our feelings, our emotional experiences, were formerly treated as "mental phenomena." We still keep the phrase "states of mind." But we might just as accurately say "states of body." There is no such thing as an emotion without its bodily expression.

A man gets angry. His breath comes short, his heart beats violently, the blood rushes to his face, his hands clench, his limbs may even quiver and grow tense. If you could subtract all these s3maptoms from a fit of anger, it is hard to say how much of the fit would still remain. They are essential parts of that "state of mind."An emotion may involve all the functions of the body—circulation, blood pressure, muscular tension, respiration, glandular activities, and the rest.Even ordinary thinking has its bodily effects, though they are not often brought to our attention. If I put an exceedingly delicate thermometer in each hand, and then give my attention to my right hand with all the concentration of mind I can muster, it will soon begin to grow warmer than my left. Somehow or other the blood circulation in it has been increased; even the diameter of it is greater, and all the tissue changes in it are going on at a higher speed.

The scientist's explanation of this is interesting. During all the history of man's evolution from a lower form, the act of thinking, he says, has normally been connected with some activity of the body. Men thought because they were going to act. Thought had its origin for the sake of action.

This association of the two became ingrained, and even now when we think in such a way that some part of the body is States of Mind and States of Body 25 concerned the automatic nerve centres begin to increase the blood supply to that part so that it may be ready for action.

A man thinks of running. The nerve centres send more blood to his legs; all the muscles used in running get an increased supply of it. A man is hungry; he thinks of a good, juicy beefsteak. Immediately more blood is sent to the muscles of mastication and to the salivary glands. Saliva is poured into the mouth, and even the walls of the stomach begin to secrete gastric juice and to prepare themselves for the digestion of the hypothetical dinner.

Now this fact has a tremendously practical application. Suppose that a man has an uneasy sensation in the locality of his heart which is due, let us say, to overeating or to gas in the stomach. But he begins to think that he has heart disease. He reads the ads" in the newspapers to learn about the symptoms—and he learns about them.A sense of constriction about the chest." Yes, that is his difficulty exactly! "Slight pain on deep breathing, palpitation of the heart after vigorous exercise"it is evidently a serious case! He begins to worry about it. Worry interferes with his sleep. It interferes also with his digestion; he does not get well nourished.

Bad sleep and bad digestion make him worse and worse. Each one aggravates the other. And all the time he keeps thinking about the heart. In the end, his thinking actually affects its condition, until he succeeds in fastening on himself a functional difficulty which may be a really serious and permanent trouble—and the whole of it can be traced back to his crooked thinking about that little pain in his chest.

This is no parable. It is the record of hundreds of actual cases. Every physician comes into contact with them.A man who keeps worrying about the state of his liver, will almost be sure to have trouble with it eventually. Indigestion can be brought on in the same way, and a long list of other ailments.The nervous system has adapted itself to the increasing complexity of modern life. It has grown more sensitive. It has become more dehcate in its adjustments. This lets

States of Mind and States of Body 27 us do a higher grade of work when we are at our best; but the machinery gets out of order more easily. The role that the psychic part of us plays in the government of the rest is increasing in importance all the time.

That is why worry is such a tremendously expensive indulgence. Worry is nothing but a diluted, dribbling fear, long-drawn out; and its effects on the organism are of the same kind, only not so sudden.No kind of psychic activity can be so persistently followed as worry. A fit of anger exhausts itself in a short time. Concentrated intellectual work reaches the fatigue point after a few hours. But worry grows by what it feeds on. It increases in proportion as it gets expression. You can worry more and worry harder on the fourth day than you could on the first. Every normal activity is strangled by it, and it is only a question of time before the man who worries hard enough will be sick or unbalanced.

But there is another side to the situation. If states of mind can hinder a man's effi-ciency, they can also help it. Positive and healthful emotions bring increased power. The simplest food taken when we are worried will often enough cause indigestion; while a man can go to a banquet and pile in raw clams, oxtail soup, roast beef, mushrooms, veal, caviare, roast duck, musk-melons, roquefort, and coffee, have a superb time, and never feel any ill effects. Not everything depends on the state of mind; but much does.There is certainly plenty of foolish philosophy connected with Christian Science, mental healing, and other kindred movements; but thousands of people have been tremendously benefited by them. This is largely due to the emphasis they all lay upon the healthful emotions, upon the positive, the believing, the buoyant, and hopeful attitude towards one's self and one's troubles.

To resolve to *'play the game" and to play it for all it is worth is the best start a man can take toward setting himself right. I know people who are really out of order, whose heart or lungs are really crippled, but who make the best of it, who have

States of Mind and States of Body 29

learned just what they can do and what they cannot do. They do not think about their troubles, and no one would even know that anything was wrong with them. They lead efficient lives. They accomplish more than most people in perfect health.

I know other men who have nothing serious the matter with them, but who fail to be efficient just because they are always turning their introspective microscopes upon their condition. They are troubled about everything they eat and wonder whether it will hurt them or not. They suspect each glass of water or milk to contain injurious microbes. They do not eat strawberries because they are afraid appendicitis may lurk there. They do not drink water at meals because they have been told it causes indigestion. They never dare let go of themselves and have a good time, for fear they may overdo. The real root of all their misery is their state of mind. If they only knew how to get at that, they could become as well off as the best of us.

But one great difficulty with people who worry is that they do not know how to get at it. They know that it does them harm, and they make an earnest resolution to stop. There is no use in that. Nobody ever stopped worrying by making good resolutions. It is contrary to the first principles of psychology; the mind does not work that way.The more a man braces himself against worry, the more worry will get its grip on him. He even begins to worry lest he is going to worry. He worries over his good resolutions, and worries because he is not living up to them.Emotions do not have handles that can be gotten hold of by main strength, by an act of the will. You cannot attack them subjectively.A man who is in the dumps can say to himself: *' Come now, brace up! Be cheerful!" but that will not make him so. What he can do and do successfully, is to make himself act the way a cheerful man would act: to walk and talk the way a cheerful man would walk and talk, and to eat what a cheerful man would eat—and after a time the emotion slips into line with his assumed

attitude. He actually bccomcs what he was been pretending to be.

We can get at worry in exactly the same manner. We can make ourselves do certain specific things. This is an objective, not subjective method.See that all the hours of the day are so full of interesting and healthful occupations that there is no chance for worry to stick its nose in.Exchanging symptoms is a vicious pastime. It always makes the symptoms themselves worse; and it is contagious: it gives them to other people by suggestion. Nothing could be more demoralizing than the way invalids, semi-invalids, and chronic com-plainers get together day after day to talk over how they feel. Crap-shooting would be a more uplifting occupation. If such cases ever get cured, it is in spite of themselves.Every man should be provided with his own smoke consumer. It is a menace to the community to have him pouring out clouds of black smoke over his unoffending friends. They will not thank him for it. And the soot may stick to them.Every man ought to have a hobby of some kind or other, one which demands a certain amount of physical work, so that when he gets,through his business there will be something interesting for him to do— something which he can talk and think about with pleasure. The business of the following day will go more smoothly, more successfully, if it is forgotten for a while. When a man is tired there is no use in keeping his head at work over business. It is the old difficulty of the bow that is never unbent.The man who will persistently ^lay well is doing something worth while; he is taking the most sensible and practical method of really getting there. He can act happy even if he does not feel so. He can stand up straight, look the world in the face, breathe deeply. He can make up his mind to tell a funny story at the table even if it kills him.

It will not kill him.

THE BODY SHOWS CHARACTER

CHAPTER V

IVTEN with thick, straight, strong necks are as a rule good fighters. They may not be quick, but they are usually tenacious. They do not know when they are "licked." Theodore Roosevelt is a good illustration of the fighting physique and carriage. Some pictures are given of him in order to show how one may maintain a "strong" carriage during the successive expression of many and divergent emotional states.

Many city business men in middle Jife have bodies that disgrace them. Everywhere you see fat, clumsy, unsightly bodies; stooped, flabby, feeble bodies; each and every degree of dilapidation and inefficiency. These bodies are not capable servants of their owners. They cannot do half the work they ought to do. They cannot give joy and pride. They do not promote self-respect.

One reason for this is their carriage. The majority of men you pass on a city street carry themselves in a slovenly manner. Observe this the next time yoa are out. Perhaps the first man you notice will be slipping along with his chest flat abdomen protuberant, head forward. The next will be fat and remind you of an inverted wedge: slim in the chest, but gradually spreading out below. With every step he takes he has to make a special effort. His weight is a costly drain upon his energy. The third man may be tall and thin, with a difference of about two inches in the height of his shoulders. He is a bookkeeper. Through his habit of always carrying something on his left arm and of bending over his desk with his weight on his right shoulder, he has gradually stretched the muscles out of shape. Not only has the position of the shoulders been altered, but there is even a slight curvature of the spine itself.

You will meet with all the variations on these three principal types of bad carriage. Not one man out of ten carries himself so as to look his best. He does not even give true indication of his real self. He possesses more courage, more personality, than he shows.

The Body Shows Character 37

But looks are not the main thing. The way a man stands and walks has bearing upon his health, upon his efficiency. If he stands always with his chest flat and his head forward, his breathing is shallow and he never makes his diaphragm do its full work. By itself, the effects of this are enough to help rob him of vigour. In the case of the man whose abdomen is so overlaid with fat that he walks clumsily, it is also true that he has an impaired blood circulation and defective respiration.

One reason for the bad carriage you see in people is that they do not know what is good carriage, nor how to acquire it. The commonest direction is, "Hold up your head." That does not hit at the real difficulty at all. A man can take any amount of pains with his head and chin, and still keep in abominable position. Changing the angle of the head does not improve things o

Throw your shoulders back," is another familiar piece of advice, and one which comes no nearer the point than the first. The position of the shoulders has hardly any effect upon the position of the body. The shoulders hang upon the outside of the body like blinds on a house. Shift their place as much as you like; you do not change the shape of the chest-cavity.There is only one way of doing that, and that is by getting the back and neck where they belong, by keeping the spine erect. This proposition is easier to talk about than to carry out. It cannot be carried out unless a man is willing to make a determined effort. Attention is what counts.

Students in military schools acquire good habits of standing and walking during the first six or eight weeks of their course. They acquire them so thoroughly that the matter needs practically no further care during later years. Constant attention is the explanation. At a military school a new student is kept watch of during all his waking hours. He is not allowed to stand, to sit, to walk, in any position except the best. Thus the whole organism gets gradually trained into the new habit.

The military student is also put through

The Body Show Character

special exercise for arms and back; but exercise is not the main factor in the process. People have the notion that exercise will make the muscles of a man's back so strong that they will pull him up straight without any thought on his part. This is contrary to facts. The back of a coal shoveller is bent, even though it is covered with coils of muscle. The truth is that a man's back tends to keep the same position in rest which it had during exercise. The coal heaver does his work with a bent back, and during rest it stays bent.

Standing straight is primarily a matter of habit, not of muscle. It depends upon a man's nervous control. The nerve centres need to be trained; and this can be accomplished only by constant and persistent attention.If a man would rigidly hold his body in good position for two months, he would probably keep on doing so always. He would have formed neural and muscular habits that would look out for the matter themselves. But there must be no times off," no let up in the forming of a habit.Now there is a simple direction that fits most cases: Keep the neck pressed hack against the collar. That will do the work.The ribs are attached to the spine in such a way that when the spine is right, they are held in the best possible position. This increases the chest-cavity, the lungs have free room to expand, the heart action is vigorous and unimpeded, the diaphragm gets a good purchase on the chest-walls.

The effect on the organs lower down is equally important. The stomach on the left side and the liver on the right side fit up close against the concave diaphragm muscle. The circulation tends to be poorer in the liver than anywhere else in the body. This is because the blood cannot flow through it directly and freely, but must be squeezed through a double network of small veins and capillaries. This is one reason why sedentary people are so likely to be bilious.

The liver is something like a sponge, and the diaphragm is like a hand that rests over it. When the diaphragm contracts vigorously, it exerts a certain pressure on the liver. Then it relaxes. This alternate con-

The Body Shows Character 41

traction and relaxation is one of the main factors in keeping the liver working well. I have known many people who were slightly bilious to remedy their trouble completely by simply taking deep breathing exercises three or four times a day.

It is clear enough that a stooping posture must decrease the eflBciency of the heart and the lungs, and injure the work of the liver. But its bad ejffects do not stop there. When the abdomen is habitually relaxed and allowed to sag forward—as usually happens when people stand badly—all the important organs inside slip downward a little; they lie lower than they should. I have often known the lower border of the stomach to have dropped two or three inches from this single cause. Just why this condition should result as it does, I am still uncertain. Perhaps it is due to a stretching of the nerves or blood vessels—but at all events, the tone of the whole system is sure to be lowered; the organs grow flabby and do their work sluggishly.

Time and again I have succeeded in curing troubles which I was assured were organic and serious just by getting the patient to stand up straight, to walk correctly, and to breathe deeply.Now it is a sad fact that simply knowing how to stand up straight will not remedy the difficulty. What counts is not the number of remedies we may have on our tongue's end, but the use we make of the remedies. Directions have been supplied. How is a man going to carry them out ? This is the most practical question of all.In the first place, he must depend upon himself. There are many braces sold that pretend to accomplish the desired results. They claim to hold the shoulders back, to hold the head up, to set the faulty position of the trunk right. But the truth is that the longer a man uses braces, the less able he will be to stand up straight.If the braces are strong enough to make a real pull on the shoulders, they are doing the work that belongs to the muscles; and that means that the muscles are getting less and less capable every day of doing it for them selves. It is the old law of use and disuse.In any case, as we have already seen, it is

The Body Shows Character 43

not the shoulders that are really at the root of the trouble. Round shoulders are the result of bad carriage, not the cause of it.The next pointer is never to exercise except in a good position. The body will tend to keep that position after the exercise is over. Visit any gymnasium you like and observe the way the men stand at the pulleys. They have no realisation of the effect it will have upon their habits of body carriage. During all exercises the body should be held in the finest position possible.

Then finally there are one or two simple exercises that have a special value for this very difficulty.

(1) Inhale slowly and as strongly as possible. At the same time press the neck back firmly against the collar. Now hold it there hard. There is no harm in doing this in an exaggerated way. The object is to straighten out that part of the back which is directly between the shoulders. This

deepens the chest.

(2) For men who are fat, this exercise is suggested:

Keep a good standing position. Draw

in the abdomen vigorously as far as possible. Hold it there a moment and let it out again. Repeat this ten times the first day, and increase until it can be done fifty times both morning and night. Every time you think of it during the day, withdraw the abdomen vigorously. This will strengthen the muscles that hold it in place.Queer as it may seem on first thought, there are times when it is a good thing to drop or "slump," as it is commonly called. When one becomes exceedingly fatigued, the blood pressure of the body is lowered. The blood tends to accumulate in the abdomen under such conditions. When the back bends forward and the chest gets flat, the ribs press upon the abdominal contents. The result is that more blood is pressed into the general circulation. Thus blood pressure is raised.The attitude of action is that of standing firmly. The attitude of contemplation and of intense attention, as well as of fatigue, is with the head bent forward and very possibly with the hand supporting the head.

The Body Shows Character 45

If a person habitually takes this position, then it is of no value when he is fatigued. Only the person who stands well usually can take advantage of this stimulus to the circulation when fatigued.

Good carriage is directly connected with a man's feeling of self-respect. If he slouches along with his eyes on the ground and his abdomen sagging, he is not in the position to have the strong and healthy feelings of self respect that the man has who stands erect, looks the world straight in the eye, keeps his chest prominent, his abdomen in, and his body under thorough control— a *'chesty" man.

If you are walking along the street and wake up to the fact that you are carrying yourself poorly, take the mental attitude of standing straight, as well as the physical one. Look at the men you meet and imagine that each one of them owes you a dollar. Put even a suggestion of arrogance into your position. Hold your head well back; look people squarely in the face. This will not only give the impression to others that you possess the power you want, but it will

actually tend to bring that power to you.

Flat chest, flabby muscles, jelly-like abdomen do not make for what we call a strong personality.

Keep the neck against the collar.

EXERCISE-ITS USE AND ABUSE

CHAPTER VI

"^rOT one man in a thousand has time to keep himself in the best possible physical condition. To do so would consume the largest part of his waking day. People who write books on hygiene have a way of overlooking this.

One book I have seen recommends that the teeth should be carefully brushed after each meal, the crevices cleaned out with dental thread, the mouth swabbed out with absorbent cotton and rinsed with an antiseptic wash. This process, it also adds, should be gone through with before retiring and on rising.

There is too much to do on other lines to permit the attainment of perfection in any one. What we want is that degree of cultivation that will enable us to live and work most intensely. We cannot spend our whole time oiling and cleaning the machine.

It is eflficiency we aim at, not perfection.

We want to find a practical middle ground, somehow, where we can get the 4?

largest returns with the least sacrifice. Sacrifices have to be made somewhere, in any case.

We have to let some things go on in a world of hard facts. How are we to decide which?

In the matter of exercise, the question for us is not: How much exercise will bring good results ? That is a theoretical, not a practical, consideration. The real question is: How much exercise is it worth while for a man to take if he wants to keep on the top level of efficiency.^

It is certain that a man cannot think and act energetically unless his nerves and muscles are in good working order. Muscles that are never used get flabby and soft; they become incapable of obeying the will promptly and effectively. The effects on the nerves that control them are equally bad. They lose their power of responding vividly. They cannot be relied upon to do expert work.

President G. Stanley Hall of Clark University calls the flabby muscle the chasm between willing and doing.

Enough exercise, then, to keep the muscles

of the body firm and sensitive is what we must aim at. For a man whose chief business in hfe is headwork, there is Httle to be gained in building up muscular tissue beyond that point. He may do it for recreation if he likes; but that is a different matter.

Many of us come to dislike the thought of exercise. The very word suggests conscientious and disagreeable quarter-hours spent with dumb-bells or pulley weights in the solitude of one's apartment, or, worse yet, on the floor of a gymnasium.

There is little use in recommending an elaborate system of home gymnastics. That would be easy to do. Hundreds of them have been recently put on the market. People often take them up with religious enthusiasm and get splendid results out of them—for a time. But I have known few who kept it up long. That does not mean that the exercise system was at fault. It simply means that it was not calculated to hold the interest. A man's enthusiasm for dumb-bell gymnastics is almost sure to wane after a while. There is nothing to keep him at it excepting will power and conscience, and they cannot bear the strain forever.

Therefore, I do not propose an elaborate system of private gymnastics. If a man forces himself to carry on exercise simply because he thinks it is his duty, more than half its benefits are lost. For a really valuable exercise is one which reaches beyond the muscles and the digestive organs; it braces up and stimulates the mind.

When a man is being bored to death, he is not deriving the most benefit from his occupation, even though that occupation may be a strenuous half-hour of chest weights.

The kind of exercise that hits the mark is the kind a man likes for its own sake; and the kind a man likes for its own sake has something of the play-spirit in it—the life and go of a good game. It will give a chance for some rivalry, a definite goal to aim at, a point to win—something, in other words, to enlist his interest and arouse his enthusiasm.

You cannot look at such exercise merely for its effects on the neuro-muscular ap-

paratus. It reaches the man's very self. Its psychological value is as important as its physiological.

The good a man gets out of a brisk horseback ride in the park is something more than what comes simply from the activity of his muscular system, or from the effect of the constant jolting upon the digestive organs. There is the stimulus to the whole system that comes from his filling his lungs with fresh, out-of-door air. There is the exhilaration of sunshine and blue sky, and of the wind on the skin. There is the excitement of controlling a restive animal. All this makes the phenomenon a complex one, something much larger than the mere term "exercise" would imply.

A man could sit on a mechanical horse in a gymnasium and be jolted all day without getting any of these larger effects.

The best forms of exercise will call the big muscles of the body into play, the muscles that do the work. This gives bulk effects. It reaches the whole system. Playing scales on the piano, though exhausting to one's self and others, does not belong to this class.

Exercise should not be too severe. Many ambitious people injure themselves through trying to accomplish too much along this line. Where the mind is already tired, the body can only lose by violent exertion, even if it is only for a few moments. Exercise breaks down tissue, exhausts nerve energy. If any good is to be gained from it, this body waste must be repaired. But when the system is already exhausted, it cannot afford an additional expenditure. A city man with a conscience is in danger of making too hard work of his exercise when he takes it at all.

Tennis is a game that nervous, excitable, overworked people like to play. They ought to avoid it. It works them too hard and too fast. Instead of resting them, it wears them out.

There is no better outdoor exercise for a city man than a game of golf. The alternate activity and rest that it provides for, the deep breathing caused by the necessary hill-climbing, the sociability of the game—all these are admirable features. Rowing, paddling, bowling, tramping—any form of recreation that brings a variety of

physical exertion and that appeals to a man's interest and enthusiasm—belong in the class of **A 1" exercises.

The fact remains, however, that a busy man cannot go riding in the park every day, nor spend an hour and a half on the golf links, desirable as this may be. He ought to have that kind of recreation—he must get it at intervals—but as a daily habit it is out of the question. From Monday morning to Saturday noon he needs to economise every minute. He wants to know what the minimum amount of time is that he can give to exercise, and still keep on the safe side of the danger line.

There are many people who keep well and who do their work successfully without ever taking any formal exercise at all. A man who looks out intelligently for the character of his food, who eats properly, attends to the demands of his bowels, keeps his skin in good order and provides himself with a decent amount of mental relaxation—^such a man can often go for a long time without any special exercise.

But a man who eats big dinners must get

exercise. So must a man who works in a badly ventilated room. So must a man who has a tendency to worry, or to constipation, or to headache. Indeed the number is very small of those who escape the need.

It is true, however, that in most cases two minutes of vigorous exercise a day would serve the merely muscular purposes. This is enough to keep the muscles reasonably hard and to keep the functions of the system in good working shape. It will have a bigger effect, to be sure, on the feelings than on the muscles, but the muscles will get what is imperative.

The average city business man without any physical impediment to fight against, can probably get along successfully on such an exercise schedule as the following:

(1) Five minutes each day of purely muscular exercise, such as can be taken perfectly well in one's room without any special apparatus. Five minutes a day does not put a great tax on one's conscience. There is every possibility of a man's being able to keep it up. This is to keep external muscles in trim.

(2) Short intervals during the day of fresh air, brisk walking, deep breathing. This can all

be secured in the regular order of the day's business. A man can easily spend as much as half an hour walking out of doors every day. This is for heart, lungs, and digestion.

(3) The reservation of at least one day a week for rest and recreation, for being out of doors, for playing games, etc. This is an essential. This is for both body and mind. A man who thinks he can get along without at least one vacation time a week simply proves his ignorance. He ruins his chances of doing really efficient work; for the mind cannot concern itself all the time with a single subject and still keep any freshness, spontaneity, or initiative. Such a man makes a mere machine of himself. He is sacrificing his personality and all that it might count for.

MEAT, DRINK, AND THE TABLE

CHAPTER VII

TITUNGER is an instinct, and an instinct is the log-book of thousands of generations before us—the record of their experiences. Hence it has some authority. It is more likely to be right than the latest health food advertisement.

But there are cases in which we cannot trust to our instincts without danger. The fact that an instinct has come down to us from prehistoric times, when men lived differently from ourselves, makes its directions occasionally out of date. It has not adapted itself to any of the special conditions of modern civilisation. It sticks in the old rut and calls as strongly as ever for satisfaction ; but it does not speak with the same authority. Our present needs may demand something quite different.

Take the case of the average child and the sugar supply. There is no doubt but that he is too fond of it. His appetite is a very bad guide in that particular matter. But the explanation is simple enough. Remember

the high value of sugar as an energy producer. Remember, too, how rarely in nature it occurs in the simple form. For our aboriginal ancestors sugar was a hard commodity to get; fruits and honey were about the only sources of supply. Yet their bodies needed it. Consequently, a strong, instinctive craving for it was developed in them—strong enough to make them ready to surmount obstacles and face danger in its pursuit.

Conditions have altered since then. We are now furnished with a practically unlimited supply—enormously beyond what we actually need. Yet the instinct remains, still loyal to the old rut. All of this throws light upon the familiar triple phenomenon of child, jam-cupboard, doctor.

Perhaps the most important changes of all, so far as the body is concerned, have come in the matter of our daily occupation —the way we get our living. The" natural" way is the primitive way: hunting, climbing, diving—forms of vigorous bodily activity. The body was intended to carry on a large amount of physical work, to be constantly exerting intense muscular effort,

Meat, Drink, and the Table 63

We do not live that way now. The conditions of our industrial civilisation have put an end to it. Machinery does most of our heavy work for us. We live by our brains. We walk a few miles a day and sit in chairs the rest of the time.

But this has not had much effect upon the character of our appetite. We are often hungry for the kind of food that would only suit a body under constant exercise. There are those among us, too, who are inclined to eat more than is good for them—to be candid—who like to stuff themselves. Now stuffing was a normal habit to our ancestors. They had to take their food when they could get it and trust God for the next meal. And it was easy for them to steal away into some quiet retreat and sleep undisturbed until the stomach had done the main part of its duty. The digestive organs, accustomed to coarse work and violent exercise, were able to cope with the situation. Ours are not. Fine head-work and coarse stomach-work do not go naturally together. Here again we meet with a special problem.

Much scientific effort has been expended of late to discover experimentally what kinds of food are best adapted to modern conditions. The results of these experiments are certainly interesting and suggestive; but whether or not they have proved all that is maintained for them is open to question.

One thing, however, they have made perfectly clear, and that is that the majority of us eat a much larger quantity of meat than we need—more, indeed, than we can get any possible good from. Meat twice a day is enough for anybody, and for most of us once a day would be better yet. There is no doubt, too, that such foods as grains, nuts, fruits, vegetables, should take a much more prominent place in our diet than they do. Beyond that, it would be dangerous to preach as yet.

No man knows exactly what kind of food or how much food another man needs unless he is personally well informed about his case—and he may not know even then. A man's own particular make-up is the prime factor in deciding questions of meat and drink. But there are several ways in V^hich one can tell pretty accurately whether

Meat, Drink, and the Table 65

he is getting the most out of his food or not. The first of these is through keeping track of his weight. Everybody ought to know what his own normal weight is—the weight at which he accomplishes the most and feels the best. The averages given in a life insurance table will serve in a rough way, but not so well as a table of one's own variations. It often happens that the optimum weight for a particular individual differs considerably from the general average.

By keeping track of the weight from week to week and comparing it with the standard, every alteration of the general bodily condition can be discovered and attended to. The time will come when every up-to-date bathroom will be equipped with its pair of scales.

Another way of discovering a defective condition of the digestive organs is to thump the pit of the stomach with the finger. If it makes you wince and double up, it shows that something is wrong.

The presence of gas in the stomach is also a sign of faulty digestion. It means that there is fermentation going on, that the process of breaking down and assimilating the foods is imperfect.Something, too, is indicated by one's state of mind. If you have a feeling of depression and low spirits without any apparent cause, it is time to inquire into the food supply and what the body is doing with it.A good digestion is a thing to take pride in. It ought to be cherished most conscientiously. The trouble with many of us is that just so long as we are not disturbed by what goes on in our alimentary tract, we abuse it outrageously. There will be a price to pay for this some time. The worm turns; and so does the stomach.

There are a few plain facts about how and when to eat which it would be worth a man's while to keep in mind, no matter how well he may feel.

If you are in a hurry, eat lightly. There is no virtue in gulping down a large meal just because it is meal-time. While the mind is actively engaged in the details and responsibilities of business, the digestive apparatus

Meat, Drink, and the Table 67

is in no condition to undertake heavy work. The blood supply is drained off elsewhere, giving all the contribution it can to the brain; and if a quantity of food is taken in, it simply remains undigested in the stomach.

Worry, hurry, unsettled mind, low spirits, all tend to delay or to stop the activities of the alimentary canal.

This has been neatly shown by an X-ray experiment upon the digestion of a cat. A certain amount of subnitrate of bismuth was introduced into its stomach before feeding. This substance is impervious to the X-rays, but is harmless to the organism. Hence it was possible to watch the action of the stomach while the digestion of food went on there. As long as the animal was kept nervous and excited, all the movements necessary to digestion were stopped.

Students who go at hard head-work immediately after meals often suffer from indigestion. So do letter carriers and other people whose meals are followed by prolonged physical exertion. Indeed, any kind of effort which forces the blood-flow away

from the alimentary region is injurious after heavy eating.

On this account it is worth a very special effort on the part of every man to compass one meal each day which shall be leisurely, uninterrupted, and cheerful. The arguments for this are not based on digestion only; they have to do with the mental health of the individual, and with the welfare of the family as an institution.

The dinner table is the centre of the family life, and the family is the social unit. The common meal draws all its members together under informal and familiar conditions, where mutual interests and companionship are especially promoted. Even if a man has no home of his own, it is his business to make himself a member of some household and to have a share in its life.

An energetic effort to leave one's work and responsibility behind, in the office or at the counter, a leisurely bath and a change of clothes, the deliberate resolution to be agreeable and to make the meal a pleasure for all concerned, even though it costs an effort— this is not only good for the digestion and

Meat, Drink, and the Table 69

the whole state of the body, but it also serves a social purpose of the greatest importance.

It is the fashion in some quarters to sniff at the pleasures of the table as if they were essentially of a rather inferior character. Perhaps they do not belong in the loftiest rank, but they are perfectly normal, and more than that, they afford a natural medium for the real interchange of ideas—^for real reciprocity. One cannot afford to neglect this fact.

The after-dinner state of mind exists only after dinner.

THE BUSINESS OP DIGESTION

CHAPTER Vill

OpHE body is like a stove. If you put the ^ wrong kind of fuel into a stove, you cannot get good results out of it. A hard-coal stove will not get along well on soft coal. It will suffer from indigestion. It must be thoroughly cleaned out, too, at certain times, or its works get clogged and there is trouble of another sort. Right coaling and right cleaning—those are important considerations if the stove is to carry on its legitimate business.

No man can be useful or eflScient in the world without proper food and without giving attention to the disposal of waste. Nearly all the diseases and most of the pains people have are related, first or last, to disturbances of nutrition.

It pays a man to know something about the way his stove works and how to give it the best chance.

As for coaling, then—What and how ought a man to eat.? The first important problem here has to do with the mouth and

its work—with mastication. No one has ever made a hard-and-fast rule for that which is of any practical value. If food is not chewed enough, there is a bad time due. If it is chewed too much, there is waste: patience and energy are thrown away. So much is obvious.

Now the purpose of mastication is twofold; first, to break up the food so that the digestive juices can get at it readily; and secondly, to mix it with the saliva of the mouth.

Food that is bolted is likely to ferment in the stomach before the gastric fluids can work their way into it. Food that is not well mixed with saliva is hard to digest, for saliva is an alkaline substance and stimulates the flow of the acid stomach juices. It is intended to help them in the despatch of their work.

Many people get into the habit of dosing themselves with a "digestive" or some other kind of medicine in order to stimulate the secretion of the gastric juice. This is a dangerous habit. If the same effect can be obtained through natural means, it is better from every point of view. The natural

remedy for faulty digestion is often simply to chew the food more slowly.

This increases the amount of saliva that mixes with it. This is not a picturesque nor exciting method of treatment, perhaps, but it often brings the right results.

Eating a dry cracker twenty minutes before meals may be still more eflScacious. No water should be taken with it and the cracker should be thoroughly chewed. The saliva that gets into the stomach by this means starts the gastric juices flowing, and by the time the meal itself arrives, the stomach is able to cope with it.

Nobody has escaped being informed by some earnest friend that it is injurious to take water with meals. The *"Health Hints" of the average newspaper are fertile with this sort of advice. There is really a sound reason at the basis of it, but it is carried too far. The trouble with the majority of people is that they drink water simply to wash down their solid food. This is a thoroughly bad habit. It cuts off the secretion of saliva; the stomach juices lack their normal stimulus.

Further than this, if the water is cold it puts a temporary injunction on the work of the ahmentary canal. The stomach is unable to carry on business again until the regulation temperature has been restored. And this takes time.

The moderate use of water or other liquids at meals does no harm, if a man takes them not as a wash but as a drink.

There are plenty of other causes for indigestion besides slipshod mastication. A faulty circulation of blood through the abdomen is one. This may be due to interference either from within or from without.

Tight clothes are the commonest form of outside interference. Not only is the blood circulation hurt by them, but the free action of the great diaphragm muscle beneath the lungs, one of whose duties is to keep the walls of the stomach kneading and churning the food contents, is hampered. Military coats, stays, tight belts—anything that really binds the body—are sure to be harmful.

It is hard to get people, particularly women, to admit that their clothes are too

tight. A pressure mark left on the skin after undressing is an infallible sign.

Internal interference with the circulation is most often due to some trouble with the liver. Anything which stops the free flow of blood through this organ dams it back into the region of the stomach and produces congestion there. A bad liver circulation frequently comes from the use of liquors, particularly from drinking on an empty stomach. If a man is going to drink liquor at all he should do so only when he eats. The evil effects and the morbid appetite developed by drinking occur largely in connection with indulgence between meals.

In a great many cases the cause of digestive troubles is to be found in a bad carriage of the body: neck forward, ribs depressed, abdomen protuberant—what has been termed the "gorilla" position. This allows a slight displacement of all the important organs of the abdominal cavity; and such a displacement, along with the reduced power of the heart and diaphragm, may work great harm. The matter of right carriage has already been discussed. The first step in getting the digestion into better shape is often the correction of this easy but villainous habit of bad posture.

Another great aid is deep breathing. After breakfast and after luncheon, as you are walking on the street, breathe just as deeply as you can ten times in succession. Then breathe normally for a minute. Then take ten more deep breaths. Do this four or five times the first day and increase it by one round every day until you are taking from three to four hundred deep breaths daily as a regular habit. This consumes no time. You do it while you are walking on the street. It improves the action of the diaphragm. It stimulates the circulation of thc blood in the head. It increases the activity of the intestinal movements. It costs no money.

Right there, perhaps, lies the chief difficulty with it. If each breath cost a man a cent, a great many more men would cultivate the habit.

Most of us take but little exercise. We sit in chairs and work with our heads. Nature intended our bodies to do muscular

work. When she did that job, she did not look ahead to the complex and artificial conditions of modern city life. But it is clear that one of the best methods we have of raising the efficiency of the bodily functions is exercise. It is especially helpful to imperfect digestion.

If a man will go to a gymnasium, or swim, or bowl, or box, or play golf, or do anything else that involves a good deal of exertion for the big muscles of the body, the whole system will respond energetically. The digestive organs will be among the first to feel the effect of the new life.

But we must make a clear distinction between what is called "general exercise'* and other forms. A man can work his hand or his throat or the muscles of his face most conscientiously without getting any benefit so far as his general health is concerned. The value of exercise is in proportion to the total amount of work done. The larger the muscles, the more work they can do. It is chiefly through using the muscles of the legs and trunk that results for the system as a whole may be secured.

Take big movements of the big muscles.

Swinging a pair of light Indian clubs may be interesting and pretty, but it does not have much to do with the health. Twisting the trunk from side to side, bending forward the back, are types of exercise that bring results. The majority of popular sports call for such movements as these. It is the big movements that count,

WASTE

CHAPTER IX

TNDIGESTION, nervous exhaustion, constipation—three of Nature's star plays when she makes up her mind to get quits with you. You cannot cheat her either. She plays the game for all it is worth.

Constipation is ten times more prevalent than are nervous disorders. I believe that more of the chronically sick are so because of this than for any other reason. It is peculiarly the penalty of city life, the price we pay for living under artificial conditions.

Any number of special causes may lie at the root of constipation, but the commonest is certainly physical inactivity—the life of the ojQSce chair and the rapid transit. The digestive organs were not planned with that in view. They are not self-sufficient. They need to be helped along in their work by the rest of the body.

Vigorous physical exertion stimulates them. The jar of hard walking or running, the stretch and twist of climbing, and swimming and heavy muscular work—all these serve to keep the digestive tract in constant activity. In the daily programme of most of us there is nothing to supply this need. Therefore the passage of food through the intestines tends to grow sluggish, and the colon and rectum are in danger of getting clogged.

That is one cause for constipation. Another lies in the kind of food we eat. We take so much trouble nowadays to have it nourishing, digestible and perfectly prepared that we often fail to give the stomach and intestines enough work to do. There is not enough bulk in the food. The walls of the intestines cannot get a good grip on it.

Food that is "predigested" is worse yet for a healthy man. It leaves practically no responsibility for the alimentary tract; and the alimentary tract needs responsibility if it is to keep in order. Idleness leads directly to incompetency. The system forgets how to take care of a square meal. "Concentrated" foods are worst of all. Eat mince pie, sauerkraut, and rarebit occasionally if you will, but give a wide berth to the steady use of concentrated foods. They

have a place in the world, but it is not that of a regular diet.

The trouble with most of the health-foods, whose boom days seem to be just passing the meridian, is that they are found wanting in two important respects. They have not enough bulk, and they lack grit; that is, there is nothing in them to irritate and stimulate the intestine-walls. The intestines need stimulation from within as well as from without. The reason why figs, raisins, bran-crackers, are good for constipation is because they provide just this.

I know two university students who tried the experiment of making their whole diet consist of predigested foods. They were preparing for final examinations and wished to secure the maximum nourishment with the least expenditure of nervous force. The experiment was decidedly successful, except for the fact that after the six weeks of intense labour their digestive organs were in such a state of inefficiency from prolonged lack of use that it took them months to get back to normal working conditions.

Then there is the practice of using laxa-

tives. It lies back of thousands of chronic cases of constipation. A man who uses a laxative to help him out of an inconvenience is not hitting at the root of the difficulty at all. The conditions that gave rise to it probably remain, and they will make trouble again. In a little while the system gets to rely on the laxative; then the habit becomes a necessity. The doses have to be made larger and larger, while their effects become less and less all the time.

No laxative—not even an enema—will work permanently. They go round in a vicious circle. They all leave their victim worse off than when he began. They make his trouble chronic. They never touch the real cause.

One man out of every ten is said to be a slave of the laxative habit.

Another sure method of achieving constipation is that of delaying to answer the calls of the system when they come. It is not perfectly easy, perhaps, to attend to the matter when the first messages from the rectum arrive. It is easier to put it off. It continues to be easier.

But after a while the nerves get tired of their ineffectual efforts and cease to prod the brain any longer. Consequently, when a convenient opportunity finally comes, there is nothing to remind one of the need. A delay habit like this leads to the most serious kinds of results. If a man kept a regular time each day for attending to the business of disposing of the waste-products of his body, the system would soon adjust itself and be ready to respond at the right moment. Regularity in this matter is essential to healthy living.

Often enough, though, the root of the difficulty lies not so much in bad habits of the body as in bad habits of mind. The way in which a man looks at himself and at the world has a lot to do with what goes on in his digestive tract. No part of the body except the muscular system is so much affected by states of mind as the digestive and excretory organs. Worry and nervousness wreck digestion. Discouragement and low spirits lead the straight road to constipation.

A man's mind may be constipated before

his body. Melancholy tends toward constipation and constipation tends toward melancholy. It is a merry-go-round draped in black.

Most people have the idea that constipation means infrequency of bowel movement. That is merely a symptom. Many men suffer from constipation who have passages with perfect regularity. Constipation is the condition which results from incomplete passages. It is due to the presence of waste-products in the alimentary canal. If there is a constant remainder there, the body keeps absorbing some of the poisons of decay from it and dumping them into the circulation. The system is poisoning itself, slowly but surely. All the symptoms show this.

A sense of fulness and pressure in the abdomen is one of them. The presence of gas—a fermentation sign—is another. There is likely to be a persistent, nagging headache—the kind that cannot be shaken off. The breath is bad, and a man feels in chronic low spirits, down in the mouth. There is a definite lessening of mental

power; the mind works at slug-pace and without any of its habitual energy. It takes a big effort to set one's self at work and to accomplish things. Besides this, the complexion is likely to be poor, the skin muddy and unhealthy looking. These symptoms are all due to the same cause: a body saturated with waste product, with poisons, which ought to have been gotten rid of. It is a villainous condition.

But there is no need of its being permanent.

THE ATTACK ON CONSTIPATION

npHE first step in the cure of constipation is to get into the right frame of mind. That may be easier said than done. Nevertheless, a cheerful and optimistic temper is the most efficacious of all remedies. "Believe and thou shalt be saved."

The digestive tract is remarkably susceptible to faith. People who suffer from constipation are often remarkably destitute of it. They prefer to believe the worst about themselves. They even seem to get a morbid satisfaction out of it. No matter how encouraging has been the outcome in other cases, they are sure there is no hope for themselves; that they are incurable.

An energetic conviction that the trouble can and will be cured counts tremendously in curing it. That is why Christian Science and other forms of mental healing often work such admirable results when applied to chronic digestion troubles.

The difficulty lies in the fact that a man cannot always control his mental attitude simply by setting out to do so. He can say over to himself, *'I will be optimistic,' several hundred times a day and yet remain most sad. He needs specific things to do; he needs to get at his problem in a concrete way.

There are a few purely practical suggestions that ought to fit in at this juncture. I have known a great number of people who have found help in taking a glass of cold water both upon rising and upon retiring. The simplicity of this treatment is its only fault.

If you have been paying very conscientious attention to your diet in the hope of knocking out the trouble that way—worry less and eat more. Stop thinking about it. Give your conscience a vacation. Your character will not suffer.

See to it that there is bulk in your food, something for your intestines really to get hold of and work on. Food which contains cellulose or other mechanically irritating substances is excellent. Bran biscuits at night are often useful in this way.

Exercise, again, is a most important forni

of treatment. The reason is the same as in other cases; it is an attempt to get back some of those conditions under which the body developed its functions.

Many of the forms of exercise prescribed for the cure of constipation are more dramatic than practical—not because they would not help if followed, but because no one will follow them. To this class belongs the following: Lie flat on the back in bed and work the head of a sixteen pound iron ball along the course of the colon, the walls of the abdomen to be completely relaxed, the movement to be made slowly, and a cheerful temper to be preserved throughout. Theoretically excellent.

Far more practical is a ride upon a hard trotting horse. This is effective because the continuous jarring of the body helps along the work of the intestinal walls. The easier the horse, the less his therapeutic value.

Rapid walking is commonly one of the effective means. This gives the same jarring motion to the abdomen. If the speed is as great as possible, there is a slight twisting of the hips with each step which keeps the abdominal organs in constant motion. And since fast walking is a form of energetic exercise, calling into play-large groups of muscles in rapid alternation, it greatly increases the movement of the diaphragm. We have already spoken of the important part played by the diaphragm in the work of the digestive tract.

Running, deep breathing, twisting and bending of the trunk, and the majority of general gymnasium exercises, are all among the normal remedies.

Such suggestions as these do not strike as deeply as the mental attitude, but they represent the concrete side of the proposition. They are practical. They give a handle to get hold of— something that a man can set himself doing; and if he goes at it in earnest and with the intention of playing the game for all it is worth, the right mental attitude is pretty sure to come too.

I remember most vividly a case that came under my direction a few years ago. It was a professional man of middle age^

conscientious, a hard worker, very much in earnest. It was easiest for him to look on the dark side of things, and he worried constantly about his own physical condition —which, for that matter, was in a pretty bad way. Heredity, he believed, was the source of his trouble; and having found this explanation he was convinced that nothing could be done for him, that his case was hopeless.

He listened indulgently to stories about other people who had been cured; but he was chiefly interested in telling about himself—the harsh measures he had submitted to; the enormous drug doses he had taken —all in vain. This he related with a sort of martyr pride. It was evident that the role of victim was not without its compensations.

The first advice he got was to take deep breathing exercises, lying on the floor of his bedroom. He had to take these in a leisurely manner, with intervals between each round of five deep breaths; and it was not until later that arm and leg movements w^ere added. Any heavy exercise brought on dizziness.

Twice a week he took a ride on a hard trotting horse. Then I set him to running, first a few yards at a jog pace and then an interval of walking, then a Httle more running. I used to watch him sometimes through a hole in the fence as he conscientiously went the rounds of the track, and I shall never forget the expression on his face. He wanted to be bored, but he knew that would be WTong—contrary to directions. So he bravely jogged along and succeeded in taking it something in the spirit in which a man takes a bad joke that he knows he is expected to laugh at.

Much the hardest thing to get at in that case was the mental condition. I knew that he could not be cured until that was changed somehow. Finally I directed him to tell a funny story at each meal of the day, with an extra two at dinner. That was because it was entirely impossible for him to control his own state of mind by willpower. He needed a handle—some objective way of getting at it. He rebelled violently at the new orders, but finally consented to make the attempt.

The Attack on Constipation 99

It was such a terrible undertaking for him that for the first few days he could not open his mouth. He forgot his stories completely. Then I made him write them down on a piece of paper and keep them in his lap for reference. When a pause in the conversation arrived he would become restless, look anxiously about, glance at his lap, summon up his courage, clear his throat and begin. The prescription was a bitter one for him; but he had promised to makc thc attempt, and before a week was out, the humour of the situation struck him, and he began to enjoy the fun. After that his recovery was sure.

Before six weeks had passed there had taken place such a change in his character that all his acquaintances noticed it. He had been suffering from constipation for years. He grew cheerful, light-hearted and approachable. The whole current of his life had turned in a different direction.

From a case like that much may be learned.

FATIGUE

CHAPTER XI

npHAT great Italian physiologist, Angelo Mosso, has given an account in his book on "Fatigue" of the arrival of flocks of quails on the seacoast of Italy on their northward migration from Africa. The distance across the Mediterranean is three hundred miles or more, and the bird covers this distance in less than nine hours, flying at the rate of eighteen or nineteen yards per second.

When the quail sights land its strength is almost exhausted. It seems to have lost the power of recognising objects, even though its eyes are wide open. Every year vast numbers of birds dash themselves to death against trees, telegraph poles, and houses on the shore.

Those that have met with no accident lie motionless on the edge of the beach for some moments as though stunned. They seem to have become incapable of fear, and sometimes even let themselves be caught by hand without trying to get away. When

they finally awaken to their exposed position, they pick themselves up suddenly and run for a hiding place. But they do not fly. It is days before they will use their wings again.

We can see effects of a somewhat similar kind in ourselves when we are exhausted. I remember a certain ten-mile bicycle race in which I was a contestant. I had fastened my watch to the handle bars in such a way that I could keep my eyes on it during the race. Before I had finished the fifth mile, I found that it was impossible for me to read the watch-hands. I saw them plainly enough, and after the race was over I could recollect how^ they had stood at certain points in the course; but at the time I had lost all faculty of getting any meaning out of them.

An incident of this kind suggests how deep the effects of fatigue strike in. It is easy to show by experiment that fatigue slows down the circulation, dulls the nerves, lessens the secretion of the glands, decreases the power of digestion, reduces the ability of the system to recover from shock or

injury, and makes the body peculiarly liable to disease.

In other words, fatigue lowers all the faculties of the body. The effects on the other parts of a man are just as important. It puts a chasm between seeing and acting; it makes a break, somehow, between the messages that come in to the brain from the outside world and the messages that go out. It destroys will-power. In every direction it decreases elSSciency, forcing the personality down to a lower level.

Fatigue is a destructive agent like sickness and death. It is a condition which in the nature of things we cannot avoid; but it is important for us to know what it is and how to deal with it if we want to keep out of costly blunders.

When we are tired out, we are not ourselves. A part of us has temporarily gone out of existence. What remains is something that belongs to a more primitive state of civilisation.

Our personalities are built up in strata, one layer added to another. At the bottom lie the savage virtues and vices of our

remote ancestors. The code of morals of cHff-dwellers and hunting tribes still holds there. At the top lie the higher attainments of an advanced society—the things that have taken hundreds of centuries to acquire. In men, patience is one of these; modesty is another; chastity, and a fine sense of justice and personal obligation belong in the list too.

Now when fatigue begins to attack the personality, it naturally undermines these latest strata first. When a man is exhausted he finds it difficult to be patient. That is not his fault. It is because fatigue has forced him back a few hundred generations. His self-control is at a low ebb. The smallest annoyances are enough to make him lose his temper.

The same holds true of all the recent character acquisitions. Many temptations are more violent and harder to resist when a man is fatigued. His moral sense is dulled. He loses the vividness of his distinctions between right and wrong, honesty and dishonesty.

We degenerate from the top down. The last thing acquired is the first lost.

Therefore, bodily vigour is a moral agent. It enables us to live on higher levels, to keep up to the top of our achievement. We can not afford to lose grip on ourselves.

The only thing to do with fatigue, then, is to get rid of it as soon as possible. As long as it is with us we ought to realise that we are not our normal selves and to act in accordance. Important questions must not be decided then. It is a bad time to make plans for the future. A man has lost his faculty of seeing straight.

It is often said that the best way of getting rid of fatigue is a change of occupation. This is usually true, but not always. A moderate degree of muscular fatigue will not keep a man from taking up something which will use his brain; and while his brain works, his muscles will rest. But there is a degree of muscular fatigue which makes head-work impossible.

The converse of this is also true. If a man's brain is used up, hard exercise is nothing but a sheer drain upon the system, not in any sense a form of rest. The central battery has run down. The energy supply

is exhausted. To force anything more out of it is to kill the goose that laid the golden eggs.

Unfortunately, a good many men have the conviction that they must keep exerting themselves all the time. They call every moment wasted which is not spent in activity of some kind, either physical or mental. Such men are taking the quickest means to burn themselves out. You cannot live well and keep happy under a constant and tyrannical sense of effort. There must be times of play, times to let up the tension, and to do easy and natural things which do not require conscious and exact attention.

Horace Bushnell, the great Connecticut minister, recognised this when he said, "Let's go sin awhile." Sinning has the advantage of being easy, and there are times when the easy thing is the right thing. A man who takes no time off for one kind of play or another, but who keeps the anxious, conscientious look on his face day in and day out, may be on the road to heaven, but he will find that the sanitarium is a way-station.

Each man has his own special manner of reacting under fatigue—^what physiologists call his "fatigue-curve." One works along steadily and evenly right through the day without any alternation in his efficiency worth recording, except that it shades off gradually during the last hour or two. Another man is unusually slow in getting warmed up to work, but once in action he maintains a higher level of productivity than the first man; and he may be able to hold the pace longer besides. A nervous man can usually throw himself with great vigour into his work. He is under way in a minute and sweeps quickly ahead of all competitors. But the chances are that his energy will not hold out long. He taps it too fast. After two hours, or less, he is likely to feel jaded and tired. His head needs a rest before he can put it to work again.

Each of these types is familiar, and there are as many variations as there are individuals. Yet men rarely take this into consideration when blocking out their day.

It is useful for the nervous, high-strung,

quickly-fatigued man to try to live by the same programme as his phlegmatic, even-tempered neighbour. The conditions under which the two men produce the best results are not identical. The man who cannot work at his best until after a long period of warming up, ought to stick to his job, when once he has gotten at it, as long as he can keep up to the high-grade level. That is the only real economy for him. On the other hand, the man who accomplishes most when he works by spurts and takes intervals of play between times, ought not to feel that he is doing wrong when he gives up imitating the steady workman. System and continuous driving decrease, not increase, his efficiency. Both men can do high-grade work, but not under the same conditions.

Every man ought to discover the special conditions of his own best work and to try to make such conditions for himself, in so far as he can. Otherwise there is a waste somewhere. Nothing is gained and much is lost through trying to run everybody through the same mould.

I have spoken of fatigue as one of the destructive agents. That does not mean that there is any harm in being thoroughly tired at night after the day's work, if only a man knows how to look out for himself. Other things being equal, the system will soon repair the waste, and by another day the man will be ready for energetic work again.

The time when fatigue becomes a really dangerous agent of destruction is when a normal amount of rest does not do away with it—when it piles up day after day, so that a man comes from his work tired and goes to it equally tired. Such fatigue as this keeps him living on a low level of efficiency. He never gets up to his own possible best. This may be because he works too hard, but it is more likely to be because he does not know how to look out for himself.

An athlete who is training for the two-mile run cannot cover the whole course every day. The physical cost of the exertion is so great that a single night is not enough to make good the waste. A man who is training for the fifty-yard dash can do several heats every day.

How much rest a man needs depends on the character of his work and on the personal make-up of the man himself.

Over-fatigue is fatigue that does not disappear before the next exertion. Overfatigue piles up against the day of wrath. This must be guarded against.

SLEEP

"^JOT one of the fundamental questions about sleep has yet been answered. What really happens when we go to sleep ? What is it that sleeps ? What is the real distinction between sleeping and waking?

We know little about the real nature of this every-day mystery. We have had to unlearn most of the older orthodox theories, and we have not yet found adequate ones of our own to take their place.

We cannot say nowadays that "sleep is fatigue of consciousness." That is meaningless. You might as well speak of the fatigue of a brook or of an electric current. We cannot even say that consciousness necessarily disappears during sleep. Certainly the brain does not stop working then. It is still capable of carrying on all kinds of complicated processes—even solving mathemtical problems or composing poems. If this is unconsciousness, it is an odd variety. And on yet lower levels it can dream.

But if it is not the brain that sleeps, what

115

is it? Certainly not the body. The body keeps working incessantly. Its activity is simply reduced to a somewhat lower level. The heart beats more slowly, the blood pressure is lower, breathing is irregular and less frequent, the muscles are relaxed, the blood supply to the brain is diminished. But there is still work being done.

Perhaps we should come nearest the truth if we said that whatever the Thing is that goes to sleep and wakes up again, it is never all asleep nor all awake. It is more or less both at once.

We could illustrate what we mean by an upright scale like a barometer-back. When the indicator is near the top of the scale, the consciousness is most active, wide awake, alert to all impressions, able to give attention without effort. As the marker sinks and sinks on the scale, we become gradually less and less aware of our surroundings, our attention flags, we cannot concentrate our minds; we are at the mercy of any ideas that drift into our consciousness. This is the condition of reverie.

Then comes a point where we fail to get

sense impressions from the outside world. The light seems to grow remote; we do not feel our clothes nor the chair or bed on which we are resting. Our thoughts become less connected and more indistinct, and in a few more minutes we have sunk into the condition we call sleep. But we have not crossed any sharp dividing line. We have dropped there by easy stages. Even now our brain may keep working indistinctly, and as the indicator rises on the scale, we begin to dream and perhaps may even hold conversations aloud with real people in the real world.

Sleep, then, is a merely relative condition, not sharply cut off and separated from waking life, any more than the ebb-tide on the seashore is distinct in its nature from the high-tide. They are different stages in the same phenomenon.

Looking at the matter in this way clears up a number of misleading ideas. One of them is that during waking hours we tear down and during sleeping hours we build up. This is true in part. But as a matter of fact, we are tearing down both day and

night, and we are always building up. The work of destruction and the work of repair go on side by side.

The difference is that we destroy faster during the day than we can build up. The spending gets ahead of the income. Whereas at night, when the activity of the body is less, when its outgo is cut down, the work of repair has a chance to get ahead. It is simply a change of ratio.

We are just beginning to discover how much really goes on in the mind during sleep. Sleep is not only the time for physical growth, but I am inclined to think that it is equally the time for mental growth —the time when the personality is formed; that impressions which have been gained during the day are worked over now and are made into a part of the sum total: that new resolutions which we have taken become rooted and strengthened then, new ideas that we have hit upon are digested and given their place in the memory. It seems to be a time when the mind sorts over its experiences and casts up accounts.

This is true in a special sense of the

impressions and impulses that come to us just as we are on the verge of sleep. This is the moment of all moments when we are most susceptible to psychic suggestion. It is almost like the state of the hypnotic subject, when every command is put into execution. A man who is ambitious for himself will take advantage of the opportunity this offers; and when he goes to sleep he will make sure that the thoughts admitted into his mind are strong and healthy thoughts— thoughts of joy, of success and accomplishment.

This is not romance. It is certain fact that a man can make suggestions to himself at this time, and that there will be a positive effect for good upon the spirit and efficiency of his life. Character is formed more during the rest that follows work than during the work itself.

The benefit a man gets from sleep does not seem to be in proportion to its length. Five minutes of sleep in the middle of the day will often give a most surprising brace-up to the system. Something happens then—no one can say just what—but there

is some readjustment, some new coordination, which may bring an entirely fresh vim and push to a man, enabHng him to make the attack on his work with redoubled vigour. This, while hard to explain, is a matter of common experience.

Dr. Morse, the great geographer, had an original way of taking advantage of a moment's sleep, and of doing it in such a manner that he did not lose time from his work. When the sleepy feeling came over him as he worked late at his desk, he would place his wife's darner in one of his hands and hold it between his knees, resting his elbow on his knees. Then he would yield to the impulse and close his eyes. But as soon as he really fell asleep, his hand would relax; and the sound of the wooden egg falling to the floor would waken him. Strangely enough, the second of sleep that he had thus secured would be enough to let him work on for another period with new energy. Then he would go through the same process again.

My father had such control of the mechanism of sleep that often he would take a five minutes' nap just before going upon the platform to deliver an important address. It gave him new strength and new grip for the effort. How he managed to do it, he was not able to explain himself.

Not many men, however, can hope to gain such a degree of control of sleep. For most of us it is still a difficult thing to get to sleep after a hard and exhausting day of head-work. Intellectual excitement fatigues us, but it does not make us sleepy. Instead, the more we work our heads the harder it is for us to sleep. The questions that have absorbed us during the day have a vicious way of cropping up in our minds again, do what we will to drive them out. We are fatigued through and through, but we are painfully wide awake.

The problem that this situation presents has not been satisfactorily solved yet. But it must be solved sometime, for it is perfectly clear that civilisation is tending more and more to make head-work the controlling factor in life. It is my belief that one of the next great steps forward will be the gradual acquisition of sleep control, so that a man can take a few minutes' rest whenever he wants it through the day.

As a general principle, it must be remembered that sleep is a non-strenuous thing. It must not be approached like an enemy to be conquered, but as a mistress to be wooed. One rarely succeeds by direct attack, but can usually succeed by indirect attack. Hence a period of leisure and quiet should with almost everyone precede the direct attempt to go to sleep. It is only under rare conditions that it is wise to go to bed directly from hard work, either physical or mental. An interval of quiet, of leisurely doing something without mental tension, is important. To let down the tension of the day, to become quiet in body and in mind, is the first essential step.

One may by several means affect the body and thus aid in securing sleep. If the head is hot, cold water applied to the face, to the back of the neck, or even to the entire head continuously for a minute or two will frequently be of a real value. Of still greater utility is a warm bath. This relaxes the entire body. The last part of the bath should be taken in water as hot as it is possible to have it, the person merely sitting in it. This will dilate all the blood vessels of the legs and thus tend to leave less blood in the head.

Gentle rubbing of the skin of the body and of the legs tends to accomplish the same result. Some people get manifest advantage from a moderate outdoor walk; some people profit by taking twelve, fifteen, or twenty slow bendings of the legs. Rapid exercise, which materially increases the working of the heart, tends to keep one awake.

There is a group of agencies which directs itself to the mind. I have already spoken of the need of relaxation. Many people can read themselves to sleep with some light novel or magazine. Others—particularly those who suffer from eye strain, find themselves wider awake the more they read, even though the reading is of the lightest character. Of a similar nature is the playing of some musical instrument. This may be effective in keeping other people awake, but one must estimate things in terms of comparative value.

There is a large series of intellectual "stunts." The utility of these I doubt. Their supposed efficacy lies in producing such mental fatigue that sleep comes on promptly. I refer to such efforts as the calculating of multiples to as great an extent as is possible to the individual. This involves, of course, a high degree of concentration. Another form is to repeat the alphabet backward until one has so learned it, then to repeat it beginning with A and next taking Z, then B and Y, and then so on until this becomes familiar—constantly seeking some rearrangement of letters, so that intense attention is involved. Thus persons have worked out extensive problems in geometry, by visualising the figures.

Then again people may be sufficiently fatigued to go to sleep and they may be quiet, but their minds will not stop working over some special problems or worrying over real or imaginary difficulties. The time-honoured problem of counting imaginary sheep jumping over an imaginary stone fence is familiar. One must imagine a large flock of sheep approaching a stone wall which has a gap in it. The wall is too high to jump over and there is only one selected gap. The gap must be so narrow that but one sheep can jump at a time. Then one must count this large flock of sheep one at a time until sleep supervenes and comes to the aid of the outraged sheep. I confess that personal experience with this particular test and others based upon the same principle has not been very favourable. My sheep seemed to be very athletic. They proceeded to find other places in the wall, over which they attempted to jump. I must shoo them back with great diligence at the same time that I am counting those that jump—and they never jump regularly —through the desired gap. My sheep are also obstreperous. Even after I have a large number securely over the fence and have counted them, I cannot then rest quietly, for these sheep in all their most earnest stupidity will endeavour to jump back. In attempting to go to sleep by this means, after ten or fifteen minutes I have found myself with rigid muscles and clenched hands, far wider awake than I wai^

at the beginning, in my futile endeavour to control the sheep of my imagination. However, it works with some people.

The fourth way which people take to secure sleep is by means of drugs. Certain drugs act promptly, and no immediate ill results are to be observed. I know of no drugs, however, that can be used continuously and that do not result in making the person dependent upon them, and which do not directly injure in some way the health or the stamina of the person taking them. My own conclusion is that drugs for the sake of sleep should never be taken except upon the advice and with the knowledge of a physician who is acquainted with the general conditions under which the person is living. Every normal person ought to be able to command sleep by means of the ordinary conditions of good health and work as already described. When these conditions are beyond the control of the person he should then take counsel of a physician.

STIMULANTS AND OTHER WHIPS

CHAPTER XIII

T TNDER the constant pressure of city ^^ life a man is always on the lookout for short-cuts. He jumps at every possible chance of getting bigger returns with less outlay of time. He wants to put in every minute where it will count. When he takes time out for sleep, he wants to do it up in good shape. When he gets in his recreation, he wants to enjoy himself to the top limit. No matter what he is doing, he goes into it for all it is worth.

This is why drugs and stimulants make such an appeal to the city man. They offer a short-cut method of getting results. They seem to give Nature a boost.

A drug will often put us to sleep sooner than we can get there unaided. If we have the "blues," we can take a dose out of a bottle and soon feel happy and energetic again. With the help of a powder or two, we can knock out a headache and manage to keep at our business without any loss of time. If we have to work extra hours, we

can keep ourselves awake and up to the game by the help of a stimulant.

In other words, what drugs and stimulants seem to promise is increased efficiency without increased cost. If this were really the case, the use of drugs would be a habit to encourage. But there is a fallacy.

Speaking physiologically, the purpose of a drug or a stimulant is to modify some function. It affects the work of an organ, but it does not affect its structure—at least, that is not what it is taken for. It forces an organ to do work which it could not do of itself: it alters the output without altering the machinery—the natural capacity.

When we put ourselves to sleep with a narcotic we are not teaching our nerves how to let go of excitement and how to regain their normal balance. They will not be in a position to do it any better another time than they were this time, and the chances are that we shall have to go to the drug again for help. When we bring about effects by artificial, instead of natural, means, the natural means grow more and more unreliable. The sensitiveness of the nerves

Stimulants and Other Whips 131

has been dulled by the powder, but the conditions that made the sensitiveness have not been touched at all. There is no cure in a drug—simply a temporary easing-up of the situation.

A great many people do not take the trouble to think into the matter as far as that. All they want is to get the immediate result; and if this can be done through a drug, they make the venture.

The use of patent powders for headache, sleeplessness, nervous exhaustion, and similar difficulties has enormously increased within the last few years. Taken in small doses and at rare intervals, these much-advertised remedies do not seem to be injurious. But a person who gets into the w^ay of using them, soon gets out of the way of sticking to rare intervals.

This is almost inevitable. As long as the powder will produce the result he wants, he is really forced to keep on using it; for the actual cause of the trouble has never been reached and it keeps making more trouble for him and demanding attention. But after the drug has been used long enough for

the system to become habituated to it, the effect grows less and less in proportion to the size of the dose. So the doses have to be increased.

There is no drug that can be taken into the system regularly without working harm. Every drug has a secondary effect as well as a primary one. The immediate effect is all a man thinks of when he takes it; but the secondary effect follows just as inevitably. It is of an entirely different nature and it is always bad.

For example, the secondary effect of most of the coal-tar headache powders is to reduce the number of red blood corpuscles whose business it is to carry oxygen to all parts of the body. It also has a dangerous effect on the heart, bringing in a sort of paralysis which makes it incapable of normal work.

The same sort of double-dealing is illustrated by every drug. The primary effect of opium is to deaden the pain-sense and to bring on an agreeable feeling of well-being which leads gradually to sleep. Its secondary effect is to stop salivary secretions

and the functions of other glands, and to stop peristalsis. The constipation that comes from opium taking is difficult to cure.

Alcohol, nicotine, chloral, cocaine, and all the rest have secondary effects of just as undesirable a character.

To put reliance upon a drug or a stimulant is evidently to put reliance upon a treacherous ally. Nevertheless, there are times when a treacherous ally is better than none. Modern city life sometimes forces a man into situations of such great strain that he is in danger of going under. The work that a fagged horse does when the whip is laid on is not normal work for the horse; but it is sometimes necessary. The load may have to be dragged a few more miles, and there may be only one way to get it done.

A stimulant is very much like a whip. What it really does is to increase a man's energy-spending power. A drug does not create the energy in the man, any more than a whip creates the energy in a horse. All it does is to turn on more current.

When a man sits down on a hornet's nest he is immediately led to expend an unusual amount of energy, but the hornet's nest did not create the energy. It was stored up in the man's nerves and muscles. The act of sitting down in the unaccustomed place simply enabled the man to spend more energy in a given space of time than he otherwise would have done.

Now there is no doubt that one of the main reasons for our being here in the world is that we may get things done. We have work on hand, work which is peculiarly our own; and whether it succeeds or not depends altogether on ourselves. There are sure to be emergencies, periods of special strain, when everything seems to come to a head and to need attention at the same time. At such a crisis as that it is out of the question for a man to stop and rest. He needs to keep awake, to keep thinking and planning hard, hour after hour. Fatigue cannot be any factor in the situation just now.

Right here stimulants have their place. They offer a perfectly rational way of bridging the crisis. They enable a man to keep tapping his supplies of energy after the system itself utterly refuses to give up any

more. This is abnormal, of com'se; but city life is abnormal too, and it requires us to do abnormal things.

But there is one fact which must be kept absolutely in mind: The stimulant does not bring any new supply of energy into the system. There is not one atom of it added. All it does is to open the conduits wider. It furnishes nothing except the chance to spend faster.

This fact has a tremendously practical bearing. It means that every period of expenditure under stimulants must be made good by a corresponding period of rest later. This is the only possible way of getting back the equilibrium.

In a long race a man cannot make a spurt and then expect to take up the regulation pace right away. He has to go slower for a while until he has averaged things up again. A man who boosts himself over a tough place by the help of stimulants is in danger of forgetting that he has made a drain on his energy-supply. He is likely to jump into his regular work again without any let-up. To do this leaves him worse

off every time he takes the stimulant, for he never really makes good his over-expenditures. He has kept drawing more and more upon his capital. Eventually he reaches the bottom and goes bankrupt.

Many cases of this kind have come under my own observation. I have had men come to me before some important event like a big convention in which they had a large share of responsibility, and ask for some means to keep themselves going at top speed during those two or three days. After a good many years of experience I have learned that it is never safe to consent to dose a man up, unless you can get him to give you his word of honour that he will give himself a corresponding vacation as soon as the special strain is over.

Time and time again men come to me afterward and beg to be let off from their promise on the ground that they feel so well that it seems useless to bother with time off. They want permission to go right back into regular work. They don't know what they're talking about—that's all.

Stimulants and Other Whips 137

Excessive expenditure needs to be balanced by excessive rest.

If a principle like this is understood, a man has a right to whip himself up with stimulants when the necessities of the situation demand it. But it is a serious business at best, and it ought not to be tampered with short of a special emergency, and then only under medical direction.

THE BATH-FOR BODY AND SOUL

CHAPTER XIV

'T^HE fundamental difference between the "■■ class of people we call "the great unwashed" and the rest of us is not really one of cleanliness. That is merely an external symbol. The real difference lies deeper and is harder to get rid of. Put a typical specimen of the "unwashed" through a Turkish bath, and you will not have changed his class. He will not yet have entered into the glorious company of the washed.

A scrupulously well-kept skin is usually associated with the possession of a cultivated taste, a susceptibility to fine and delicate things, a degree of self-respect which is more than skin deep. The unwashed are the people who have no such perceptions.

In her opening address to the students of Bryn Mawr college last fall. President Thomas brought out this point effectively. "In our generation," she said, "a great gulf is fixed that no democracy or socialistic

theories can bridge over between men and women that take a bath every day and nien and women that do not."

And she went on: "It is the difference of which bathing is a symbol that makes marriage between people of different social habits so disastrous." A man's bath-habits, it seems, point back to his ideals of life, to his standards of culture.

The real reason for taking a daily bath is not to keep clean. A bath once a week would answer such needs well enough. As far as the actual demands of health go, we could doubtless get along on even less. The reason is psychological. Not for the body, but for the soul.

The skin is what separates the individual from the universe. It is a line of demarcation. In a certain sense it is the boundary of a man's personality. It serves not only for protection, but also for information. All the knowledge we have of the world outside ourselves comes through the medium of the skin. The embryologist has shown that all the organs of special sense, sight, hearing, and the rest, are simply develop-

The Bath—For Body and Soul 143

ments of the outer or skin-layer of the embryo. The skin deserves respectful consideration.

From the millions of delicate nerve-endings on the surface of the body, a continual flow of messages is carried along the nerves to the brain. Even where the messages are too minute to be distinguished, they settle for us what we call our general state of feeling—whether we feel well or feel dull, or out of sorts.

The more scrupulously the skin is looked after, the more responsive it will be to the stimuli that it gets from the outside world, and the more accurate and well organised will be the information which passes on to the brain.

A cold bath in the morning raises the level of our mental activity. It wakes us up, it increases the supply of energy. A bath after the close of the day's work means that we have put off the old man with his deeds, that we have left the office with its business behind and are prepared for something else. It is an act of respect to our personality.

The value of any special variety of bath

depends upon a man's own constitution. Nothing could be worse for some people than a cold morning plunge. Indeed, the very people who are apt to make this habit a matter of conscience, are the ones who will probably get nothing but harm out of it. The thin, nervous man, whose greatest danger lies in living too energetically, is the very man who will force himself heroically into the morning tub. On the other hand, the man who is hampered with an excess of fat and a sluggish brain will probably stay comfortably in bed until breakfast time. This is unfortunate.

What really determines the value of the cold bath to a man is the kind of reaction which follows it. In some cases this is too large. The cold in such cases is too great a stimulus and the ultimate result is great depression.

The cases are more frequent where the reaction fails to come at all. The heat-making power of the body is not great enough to respond to the shock. Instead, the muscles grow stiff, the skin gets blue, and the teeth chatter. The constitution of

The Bath—For Body and Soul 145

the man was not made to stand such violent treatment.

In a normal case the first effect of the cold water is to take all heat from the surface of the body. The small arteries and capillaries in that region are suddenly contracted and the blood is driven away. But this is immediately followed by a vigorous rallying of all the body forces. The muscles begin to contract and expand rapidly, producing an increase of heat; the blood rushes energetically through the whole system, respiration is deeper—the whole activity of the body is toned up to a higher level.

Putting the case formally, a normal reaction depends upon five things:

(1) The Suddenness of the Bath, —^You prevent any good results if all you do is to cool the water gradually, so as to make the process easier. That will simply chill the body.

(2) The Temperature of the Water. —This must be suited to each man's reacting power. Some people can stand a plunge into ice water without any harm; but it would send others galley-west.

(3) The Temperature of the Man, —^If the

body is already chilled, it is probably not the right time for a cold bath.

(4) Muscle-activity, —Shivering is one way in which the muscles respond to the shock. Vigorous rubbing of the skin, kicking, or any other kind of quick exercise for arms and legs, hurries things along and makes the reaction more complete.

(5) Habit. —Tho man who is accustomed to cold water baths will probably have a more effective reaction than the man whose body is unprepared for it. It takes time to get the habit, and a man cannot judge fairly of the value of the bath for himself until he has given it a fair trial. Do not be too severe with yourself at the start. A cold sponge over a small area is a good means of getting the thing under way.

So much for cold baths. The hot bath has almost a contrary effect. For a moment to be sure, there is a contraction of the surface blood vessels, but this is immediately followed by a relaxing of the muscles that control them, and the blood vessels become greatly dilated. The skin gets full of blood; the heart beats faster. In order to keep th^

temperature of the body down to normal, the sweat glands begin to work vigorously.

The special use of the hot bath is to draw away the blood from some congested part, such as the head; also, to relax the tension of the system. A man sometimes cannot get rest just because he is nervously exhausted. A hot bath may bring him exactly what he needs.

There are a great number of special varieties of baths, each of which hits certain conditions. On account of the close connection between the circulation in the back of the neck and that in the nose and brain, it is found that cold applications on the neck are a help in nose-bleed. A headache can often be reached by cold-and-hots to the same place.

Bad circulation in liver and kidneys can often be remedied by hot applications to the surface of the body nearest those organs, and other disturbances in the body cavity can be affected by the same means. Everybody knows the value of local applications in the case of a sprain or some other inflammation. A dash of cold water in the face will often knock out a congestion in the brain accompanied by dull headaches and niake it possible for a man to think clearly again.

But after all, the most practical value of the bath as an institution, is the psychological one. When a man is fagged out, a good bath will bring back his energy and change his state of mind. The increased thoroughness of the circulation, the clearing of the brain, the stimulus to the countless nerve terminals in the skin—all these effects have a distinct bearing on those general feelings of health and well-being which make joyful and efficient living possible.

People who are down with the "blues" have often gotten over them by taking the right kinds of baths. Much pessimism has been put out of business by this rather unpicturesque means. Much more still awaits treatment.

The only difficulty is that the method is so simple.

PAIN-THE DANGER SIGNAL

CHAPTER XV

TF YOU have a pain you are conscious of it. If you are not conscious of it, the pain does not exist. The cause of it may be there still; but pain itself is an affair of consciousness and nothing else.

In trying to find out what pain means and how to treat it, it is necessary to keep this in mind. We tend to act all the time as if the pain itself were the bottom fact; whereas in reality it is only a sort of indicator. The bottom fact lies deeper. If a man has ether given him, he no longer has any pain; yet the conditions that gave rise to the pain have not changed at all.

Pain is like a danger signal on a railroad. It is put there for the purpose of attracting attention. Something is wrong on the track —a washout or a wreck somewhere, that blocks traflSc. There are two ways of treating the signal. One is to cover it up—• to act as if it were not there. The other is to clear the track.

You can treat pain in the same way. You can crowd it under with drugs so that you will not be aware of it, or you may try to set right whatever the indicator told you was wrong.

When a man is trying to get rid of a pain he always ought to ask himself whether he is striking simply at the pain itself or whether he is getting at the underlying cause.

There are times when it is perfectly right to aim at the pain, It may be intense— the kind that drives everything else out of your mind, makes thinking impossible; and the cause may be too deep to get at quickly. Perhaps some mportant work must be carried through; it may be essential for a man to stick to his job a little longer. In a case like that, no one could blame him for giving the knockout to his pain sense.

He does this, however, at his peril. He ought to realise the fact. From that moment on he has assumed absolute responsibility for the conditions, whatever they are, that gave rise to the pain. When the pain itself is not present any longer to remind him that something is wrong, he is ini

danger of forgetting it, for he has nothing but his memory and his will-power to depend upon. The danger signal was set and he has deliberately run by it. He may be able to take his train a little farther, but the track has not been repaired, and if nobody keeps watch of things, there will be a "smash up."

A headache powder does not hit the cause of the headache any more than a laxative hits the cause of constipation or a spoonful of pepsin the cause of indigestion. You have cut out the symptoms, but the root of the trouble is still untouched. It is a root that will keep on sprouting, too.

Pain is associated with things that are harmful—with the forces of destruction. That relation is a constant one. Without the warning of pain we should have no means of learning at first hand what sort of experiences were not good for us. We could cram ourselves with green fruit and never discover that there was anything to be avoided in such a diet. Pain teaches us differently; and its lessons are not forgotten over night.

It is a theory of biologists that pain-sense

was the earliest development of conscious life. Sensation first came to some primitive invertebrate in sharp stinging flashes— sense messages that had a positive effect upon its actions. "Stop, quick," they directed, or "Let go," or "Don't eat that again"—signs for contraction, or rigidity, or flight. An animal that responded to these flashes had a better chance of living and producing offspring than one that did not. It was for the good of the race that pain entered into its experience.

Pain has never been meaningless. It always points somewhere, tells something; and if we dare put the extinguisher on it, we must not fool ourselves into thinking that it is the end of the matter.

As a general thing, the pain points pretty directly to its cause. You can usually put your finger on the root-trouble. When you have a burnt hand, you do not need to ask yourself where the pain comes from, nor what it means.

But this does not always hold. It occasionally happens that the relation between the pain and the cause is complex and hard

to trace. "Reflex irritation," physiologists call it. A headache usually belongs to this class. It may be due to any one of a hundred causes, and the one it is finally followed back to may have seemed the most improbable of all.

I have met with cases in which chronic headache of the most aggravated type was caused by flat feet. Yet there was no sign of pain in the feet themselves, and the person had never suspected that there was any connection there. Even a physician could not be sure of it, for often enough flat feet do not seem to have any effect on the general health. But in these cases, when the diflS-culty was corrected, the headache completely disappeared.

It is not quite clear why this should be so. Perhaps the spreading of the arch had resulted in a stretching of the nerves of the foot, and this constant tension may have reacted on the brain.

I know the case of one woman of great executive ability who wa5 a nervous invalid for years without anyone being able to account for her condition. She had to give

up her work completely. She was practically confined to a single room. She was supplied with plates for her feet. It turned out that the cause of her trouble lay exactly there, and her recovery followed so quickly that it was hard to believe it.

Reflex irritations may come from diflSculty in the digestive tract; they may come from a bad condition of the teeth or from some slight displacement in the reproductive organs—in short, from any part of the body. So small a matter as the constant pressure of a corn may give rise to serious disturbances in the intestines or the head.

Perhaps the eyes are the commonest source. Strain in the eyes is hardly ever felt there first. Instead it gives rise to headaches. A man's eyes may keep him in perpetual misery without his ever so much as suspecting it.

These connections between the reflex irritation and ks real cause are most perplexing and mysterious. They often seem illogical—^you cannot predict them in advance.

There is only one way of discovering the actual cause and effect relation, and that is

elimination. If I have no clue to a persistent case of headache, the only thing for me to do is to make a thorough and detailed examination of the whole body in order to detect any and every condition which might possibly account for the trouble. One by one all these conjectured causes must be eradicated. There is a good chance then that the actual cause will finally be hit on. It is my opinion that every man ought to have himself carefully examined once a year by a skillful physician who can be relied upon to give him trustworthy advice.

He owes this to himself. A man has no right to be wasting his energy or cutting down his supply when he could just as well have an abundance of it. Pain is costly. It unfits us for giving attention to other things. It keeps us on a constant strain. It destroys eflSciency.

Simply to blot it out of the consciousness is at best a makeshift. To find the real cause and to correct it may be a long and tiresome process, but in the end it is the only economical course of action.

A good engineer pays attention to thf ganger-signal.

VISION

CHAPTER XVI

/^NE of my friends, a professor in an eastern university, has for thirty years suffered from almost constant headaches. These vary in intensity from day to day, from week to week, but they are rarely absent. He goes to sleep readily but generally awakes in the middle of the night, and is prone to lie sleepless thereafter. He has had constant difficulty with his stomach, and periods of nervous exhaustion when he could do very little work have been frequent.

As a result of this constant pain and the nervous exhaustion, his own personal reaction to life is much of the time sad. His philosophy is deliberately optimistic, but during a great part of his life it has to yield to the state of his feelings.

My friend tried many remedies. For a year he was under the care of a physician who put him on an exclusively meat diet. With this there seemed to result a temporary improvement, but it was not per-

manent. He tried long periods of outdoor rest and exercise, and he found that mountain cHmbing and the Hke would always help him markedly. But the improvement was usually of short duration, and upon returning to work his old pains and disabilities would reappear promptly.

He next fell into the hands of a specialist, who operated upon him for piles. This specialist said that all his other symptoms of ill health were merely reflexes from this trouble. But the results, so far as general health and feeling were concerned, were negative.

For a period he was given the modern mechanical massage by means of electric machines, and his general health was slightly bettered; but no profound change, no cure of the headaches resulted. One physician put him on tonics, such as iron and strychnine, but without achieving any generally good effect.

At the age of thirteen my friend had had a partial sunstroke. One physician thought that his constant headaches might be due to permanent dilatation of the capillaries of

the brain, induced at that time; but an examination made by a specialist in nervous diseases contradicted this opinion. Applications of cold to the head and to the back of the neck failed to reduce the symptoms. Hence dilatation of the cerebral capillaries was manifestly not the cause of his ill health. Lastly his eyes were thoroughly examined (they had been superficially examined before) and glasses were prescribed. There was no immediate change and it seemed as though the search for health were again to result in failure. But then slowly an improvement began, and in the course of a few weeks it was very real. Presently, however, his general condition again began to deteriorate. Then it was observed that on one of his eyehds was a minute growth, which pressed upon the eye and changed its shape about one three-hundredth of an inch. The removal of this growth acted like a magic wand. For a short time he seemed perfectly well. He enjoyed life; his work was a pleasure in itself, which had not been the case for years. His digestion was good, and he slept well. But he soon

began to go back. Then repeated examinations showed that his eyes are undergoing a rather rapid change in shape, and until this is completed constant readjustment of glasses will be necessary.

I have given this picture somewhat in detail because, with many variations in particulars, it represents the experiences of unknown thousands. Probably one-quarter of all the educated people in America suffer from disturbances of various kinds, which are more or less due to eye strain.

This eye strain in a large number of cases creates an extraordinary and altogether not to be expected general condition of the body. Dr. George M. Gould of Philadelphia, one of our most brilliant physicians and writers, has in five volumes called attention to these general effects of eye strain with such force as to secure the assent of most thoughtful medical men, by showing that the serious disturbances of life in such men as Carlyle, Huxley, Wagner, and a score of others, were occasioned by strained eyes.

It frequently happens that persons suffering not only from headaches, but also

backaches, sometimes indigestion, and even hysteria—are cured of these troubles through the use of simple spectacles. Professor Schoen of Leipsic reports the case of a girl with epileptic seizures which were due to eye strain. He says that the constant effort on the part of the child to bring the two eyes into uniform working condition, in the course of time brought about nervous disorders of an intermittent character and finally resulted in permanent disturbances in the brain. At first thought all this appears to savor of quackery. It sounds as though these were impossible associations, but they have been proven facts.

How is it possible that strain upon muscles so small as those of the eyes can produce such tremendous disturbances of the whole organism ? If I should seriously overwork one of the small muscles of my forearm, for example, the one that moves one of the fingers, it would become lame and sore; but it would be difficult for me by means of such overwork to produce constant headache, backache, nervous exhaustion, and indigestion. And yet these symptoms are

constantly associated with eye strain. It is true that by persistent overwork of the muscles of the hand, people do get into disordered conditions—for instance, typewriter's cramp and telegrapher's palsy; but these disorders do not seem to involve anything like the upsetting of the whole system, that complete nervous exhaustion, which is the result of eye strain.

The reason for this tremendous result of eye strain appears to be at least partly this: The effect produced is not due so much to the size of the muscles involved, as to the relation which those muscles bear to the vital parts of the human machinery. The pictures that are made in our eyes, and that are always being translated into nerve currents and reported to the brain, form the foundation for our thinking. They constitute a far larger factor of the brain than the mere activity, and through interference with it many of the other organisms are disturbed. Constant exhaustion and strain of these visual centres frequently causes disturbances of the most extensive character.

We might imagine a case in which those muscles that move the fingers would play a somewhat equally important role—from the standpoint of mental operations involved—as the muscles of the eyes. Take the case of a blind man who does extensive reading with his fingers and who is engaged in work that requires the constant detection of small differences by means of his fingers. Under such conditions we should expect that a derangement of the muscular apparatus of the fingers would have a far more serious result upon a man's organism as a whole, than would be effected in those of us who do not use the fingers in a way that is so directly related to intelligence.

The strain of civilisation rests heavier upon the eyes than upon any of the other bodily organs. This is not because vision is more important to civilised man than is any other sense, but because man's eyes in a civilised community are used differently from what they are used in savage

life. No other part of the body has had the emphasis upon its work changed so greatly as has the eye. The savage had to look at near things and far things, at large things and small things, equally—while modern man reads.

The capacity for seeing type belongs to the normal eye, and it is only because we have tasked this capacity to a tremendous degree and for considerable periods every day, in order to distinguish the small differences in these black marks on white paper, that there exists this strain which is producing deterioration of the civilised eye. People with good eyesight among us have as good vision as the savages possess. This has been repeatedly demonstrated. But the percentage among us of those suffering from astigmatism, shortsightedness, and longsightedness is indefinably greater than it is among them. There is another difference between the civilised and the savage use of the eye. The civilised man will look for long periods at things which are at close range. Even when he is not reading, he will not see anything farther removed than the wall of the room—which is but a few feet away. The savage, living most of the time out of doors, has usually a long focus and he only occasionally uses the short focus. The house-living man most of the time uses the short focus, much of the time the exceedingly short focus of fifteen to eighteen inches, and only occasionally the long focus of the open. It is found that deformities of the eye increase from year to year during school life, thus showing that they are acquired and that the school is responsible for making them. Approximately one-third of all the children in the upper grades of the elementary schools have eyes which rather seriously need correction by means of spectacles. In view of the fact that the most serious results of eye deformity and eye strain are not indicated by eye pains, how may one tell whether or not it is the eyes that need treatment? There is only one way to do:

!7o The Efficient Life

Whenever there are headaches or backaches, interferences with digestion, and nervous exhaustion—^which symptoms are not clearly traceable to and curable by other definite measures—the eyes should be examined. They are peculiarly vulnerable and they must be suspected when there exist symptoms of the kind that I have mentioned which cannot be traced wholly to other sources.

What about reading on the cars.? I think this question must be viewed in a common-sense way. For example—personally, I read on the cars most of the time, because it is practically the only time that I have for reading; and reading is of such importance to me that I am willing to incur the danger of overworking the eyes in order to get the reading done. But we can safeguard our reading on cars and trains in two ways.

(1) We can select for reading that book or magazine which has clear type, good margins, and lines sufficiently short and far apart so that when the eye travels from the end of one line to the beginning of the next, it will not be apt to fall on the wrong place. By giving attention to these points, we are able to read with but a fraction of the strain which otherwise such reading w^ould involve. The strain of reading in a subway, by artificial light, or on a train at night, when paper, type, lines, and setting are good, is not nearly as severe as when opposite conditions obtain.

(2) There is another thing that we can do, and that is to select for reading on the cars those books that necessitate more study than they do reading. Some articles and books w^e skim over and race through: We digest them faster than we can read them. Other books require slow reading; one must repeatedly study and think over what has been read, or follow out side lines of suggested thought. This is the type of book for reading on trains—the book that requires study and thinking.

A little scheme which has been of great service to me is that of cutting up books which I want to read, so that they may be carried in the pocket one part at a time. The type of modern newspaper and its subject matter are not such that I want to spend all my time on the cars in reading literature of this kind. But by the plan of taking books and cutting them into parts, the total amount of good literature read by me in the course of a month has been about doubled. I confess, the first time that I stuck my knife into the back of a well-bound volume, I felt as though I were committing sacrilege, for I love and reverence books; but in view of the great profit that I have derived from this method of conducting my reading, I now do not hestitate to employ it.Sometimes I see women on the cars reading through their veils. They should give up either the reading or the veils.A practical thing when reading is to look up and off for a moment every little while. This relaxes the strain under which the eyes are working when they are focussed at short range.

Another point to be kept in mind is that while our eyes are adjusted to outdoor light, this is always reflected light. A direct light injures them. Our eyes can bear the brilliant illumination of sunshine, but they are hurt by having even a sixteen candle power electric light shine into them directly. It is these irritating streams of light that do harm, rather than the general flood of light. This is because the pupil of the eye adjusts itself so as to admit light in proportion to the general illumination, and one irritating stream of light will not serve to contract the pupil sufficiently. Hence it is particularly important for us to avoid reading or doing anything else in a position where a bright light shines directly into the eyes.

The only good plan of lighting a room artificially is to use reflected light. That is, the electric bulbs should be so arranged that the light is thrown upon the ceiling, in which case the brilliant carbons are not directly visible to persons in the room. This method requires more light, but it saves the eyes. Light is never pleasant nor safe for the eyes when one can directly see its source.

When the eyes are fatigued from long use, a cold bath to the face—and particularly a cold washing of the eyes—are useful. But the main thing is to use the eyes reason-ably, to secure glasses which will stop the strain or abnormal action of the eyes, and also to see that they do not become disordered.

Disorders of the eyes not merely affect the rest of the body, but the eyes themselves in many cases act as a sensitive barometer with reference to the conditions in the rest of the body. People with weak eyes will be far more apt to have eye pains when they are suffering from indigestion or overwork, than when normal conditions of health obtain. In the case spoken of at the beginning of this article, the eye trouble was always an indication of the general health. Therefore, it is most important that people who experience difficulties with their eyes should keep themselves in good general health.

VITALITY—THE ARMOUR OF OFFENCE

CHAPTER XVII

'IpWO men undergo operations of the same character in a hospital. The same surgeon does the work. The conditions are identical. Equal care is exercised in each operation, and each is successfully performed. Yet one man recovers, the other dies.

There is a tremendous business pressure which does not let up for months. It puts men under terrible strain. One man goes to pieces and his business is wrecked. He cannot keep the pace; he loses control of himself. His rival has no better brains than he—perhaps not so good—^yet he pulls through successfully.

We say that there is a difference in vitality; that one man has more of it than the other.

I once saw a man in a hospital who was suffering from five fatal diseases; and yet he would not die. He had kept on living year after year in spite of everything. He refused to succumb.

We find the same thing illustrated every

day. In a shipwreck there are many who seem to give up their lives without a struggle, without any power to resist. Others cling to an open raft for days without food, almost frozen, constantly whipped by the waves; but for some reason or other they survive. The vitality in them is strong.

Notice how rapidly and surely one man recovers himself after a nervous breakdown, while another drags along through years of semi-invalidism. Notice the results upon two men of a long, cold drench of rain. One of them comes down with pneumonia; the other suffers no ill effects. How is it to be explained.?

He has a reserve somewhere, an inner power of resistance, an aggressive something that will not be downed—and we call it vitality. A man cannot have a more valuable asset than that. It means joy instead of dumps, success instead of failure, life, perhaps, instead of death.

There are different ways of looking at disease. The simplest way, the most primitive way, is to look at it merely as something to be cured. This explains the power of

Vitality—The Armour of Offence 179

the medicine man, the miracle worker. To cure disease is what we constantly ask of a physician to-day. But after all, this is a mere repair work; it is like patching up a leaky boiler. It is necessary—no one doubts that; but from the most advanced point of view, its place is restricted. It is no longer the all-important thing.

A much larger work is that of prevention. In recent years we have begun to realise this. We try to provide such an environment for a man that disease cannot get at him. We provide good ventilation, we purify the drinking water, analyse the milk, work out problems of sanitation, kill off the germ-bearing mosquitoes. It is the distinctively modern attitude toward disease.

But there is another way of looking at the matter. It has to do with the vitality of a man; it is internal, not external. If the external conditions of a man's life are important, the internal conditions are still more so. If a man is so full of vitality, of resisting power, that he beats off every onslaught of disease, he is better off than the man who keeps well only because he hag built a stockade about himself and Hves inside it.

One can easily picture a town protected by every safeguard of sanitary science, furnished with germless food and distilled water, on every side completely shut off from danger. Yet that town might contain a most weak and puny set of people—people who lacked power, vigour and health, and were entirely unable to do hard work. They might have to be constantly fighting against breakdowns; they might have no capacity for enjoying life.

Vitality is not simply freedom from disease. It is something far more fundamental in a man's life than that. It is usually the men of tremendous vitality who exert an influence upon the work of the world. They are the men of power. We can all pick out business and professional men who have gone to the top because of their vitality, their ability to do things, to push, to stand strain.

It is commonly supposed that the bigger a man's muscles, the more vitality he must have. That is absurd. Some of the most

muscular men I have known have gone under because of deficient vitality. They had built up tremendously powerful muscles on the outside of their bodies; but they lacked the inner power—resistance. Many of the strong men who go on exhibition have sunken eyes, drawn cheeks: they show the effects of the vital strain under which they live. They are constantly *' too fine." They are deficient in the kind of strength that counts.

It is true that to do a certain amount of physical exercise is one of the ways of conserving vitality; but it is not the most important w^ay. The problem goes deeper than that. It involves a great deal more than the muscular system. It is a matter in which the whole personality of the man, his body and his mind, are involved.

Vitality depends on two things: what a man inherits from his parents, and what he does with himself—his habits of life.

It is not in his power to control the first. If he comes into the world with generations of city life behind him, his vitality inheritance will not be the best. There is a good

deal in the old saying about the need of returning to the soil every third generation. Vitality appears to be in inverse ratio to the number of years the family has lived away from the soil. The children of parents who have led the nervously intense and exhausting lives of cities are likely to be delicate and nervous, and without the ability to stand even an ordinary amount of wear and tear. No attention to hygienic living, muscular exercise, and the like, can make up to them for this deficiency in their

inheritance.

Vitality is not a thing that can be created. If the organism does not possess it, there is nothing for a man to do except to learn how to get along as best he can with the least possible outlay of energy.

But most of us are not in that situation. We have vitality enough if we will only make the most of it—learn how to develop and stimulate it. That is the practical problem. We have to put up for better or worse with our inheritance, but the use we make of that inheritance rests with ourselves.

Maximum vitality and maximum eflSciency

are tied up with each other. What makes for one makes for both. To learn how to attain one is to learn how to attain the other.

Physical conditions are important— healthy muscles, good digestion, normal weight, and the rest; but they need not be taken up in detail here.

The real heart of the problem is psychological. We are just beginning to understand the part that good thinking holds in good heath. Our thoughts are just as real a part of us as are our bodies. A man who persists in thinking unhealthy thoughts can no more keep sound and healthy in body than a man who violates all the physical laws of his nature.

A man's mental attitude is fundamental. It is a well-known fact that the number of deaths in an army defeated and under retreat is enormously greater than in an army upon a victorious march. The mental attitude of defeat, of discouragement, lowers the resisting power of the individual. It predisposes him to disease. The whole tone of his system is let down. His body becomes a fertile seeding-ground for infection.

The aggressive, the positive, the confident state of mind is the one that wins out over obstacles. A man who keeps on the defensive all the time, dreading danger, fighting against bad influences, avoiding disease, not only wastes an enormous amount of energy but also lessens his own chances. It is not the defensive attitude that protects a man.

It is useless to say "I will not think of this thing." No man can do that successfully. The man who piously resolves not to worry about his liver trouble will worry about it all the more. He cannot help it.

The normal way, the efficient way, is to turn one's thoughts to something worth while—^to fill the mind with healthy thoughts. This is sound psychology. You cannot drag a thing out of the mind; but it will go of itself if you put something else in its place. A determined pursuit of good thoughts, of healthy thoughts, is the only means of getting rid of the other kind.

Carlyle talks about the Everlasting Yea. To live the positive life—the life of affirmation—is to live the life that carries on efficiently its part in the work of the world.

GROWTH IN REST

CHAPTER XVIIt

/^^ROWTH is predominantly a function ^"^ of rest. Work is chiefly an energy-expending and tearing-down process. Rest following work is chiefly a building-up and growing process. Work may furnish the conditions under which subsequent growth may occur, but in itself it is destructive. By work we do things in the world, but we do not grow by work. We grow during rest. Rest is not the only condition of growth. It is, however, one of the essential conditions. It is peculiarly a topic which needs discussion in these days of concentration.

We seek concentrated food. We seek concentrated reading; the day of the three volume novel has passed. We demand that the world's news shall be epitomised. We demand that our writing shall be taken down in shorthand and written by machine. We demand that business shall be done by telegraph, telephone, or wireless. We demand that our expresses shall travel fifty

miles an hour or more, and that while on the expresses we shall be able to economise time by having stenographers and libraries. We read on the cars. The habit of reading during meals is growing.

All these concentrated activities, these ways of doing more work in less time, of shortening the period between thought and action, between the conceiving of an idea and its working out into the real world—or perhaps more truly the visible world, because the real world is the thinking world—make immensely for world achievement. But they do not make for growth of the self—they tend to dwarf the individual by sapping his power.

I might caricature this aspect of the times by taking a splendid frame and then pasting on some neutral background within this frame pictures of the world's masterpieces. The pictures should be fitted as closely as their forms permitted. They should be cut in outline, so that no picture had a background. Every bit of background must be fitted with some other picture. Every inch of space should be

economised by filling it with some beautiful, worthy thing. In a frame measuring three by four feet I could have a large portion of the world's masterpieces in representation. But it would give me neither happiness nor any true conception of these masterpieces, for none would have setting or margin.

Proper setting and proper margin are essential to every work of art. So if life's work and life's thinking are to result in growth, they too must have their margin, their proper setting, their opportunity for assimilation.

During the day the chief work of the body is done, but during the night the tissues grow more than they do during the day. The food is worked over, the muscles are built up, the brain tissue is restored, the vacuolated nerve cells become refilled and their crinkled borders become smoothed and rounded. This is margin, this is setting. It is the working up into the subjective self of the food and the results of the objective day's work.

The process is not less necessary with reference to mental work. The student

who spends all of his available time in the acquiring of facts misses the chief end of study. Wisdom does not consist in a knowledge of facts, but in their assimilation —^just as art does not consist merely in form and colour, but also in margin and setting. Our facts need assimilation. They need to be worked over into the tissue of our mental life. The daily emotions, the struggles, the ideals that come to us need to be worked over into the self. This occurs chiefly during quiet, during rest. The man who has no quiet and no rest assimilates relatively little. A man's experiences must be turned over and thought about. A man's ideals must be dreamed over and dreamed out. It may be true that sleep bears somewhat the same relation to mental growth that it does to physical growth, that thus partially or even entirely in an unconscious way the facts of daily life are worked over into the tissue of character. It is certainly true that we often awake in the morning after a good night's sleep and find problems solved, the mental atmosphere clarified in fi way that is altogether surprising, an<J

which is not to be accounted for apparently merely by our being more rested. We know that the brain is not wholly inactive during sleep. We know that there are psychic processes going on of one kind or another. I do not know what direct evidence could be procured to prove or disprove this hypothesis. It does seem, however, to fit in with very many well-established and otherwise not adequately explained facts. The best work that most of us do is not begun in our oflSices or at our desks, but when we are wandering in the woods or sitting quietly with undirected thoughts. From somewhere at such times there flash into our minds those ideas that direct and control our lives—visions of how to do that which previously had seemed impossible, new aspirations, hopes, and desires. Work is the process of realisation. The careful balance and the great ideas come largely during quiet, and without being sought. The man who never takes time to do nothing will hardly do great things. He will hardly have epoch-making ideas or stimulating ideals.

Rest is thus not merely in order to recuperate for work. If so, we should rest only when fatigued. We need to do nothing at times when we are as well as possible—^when our whole natures are ready for their very finest product. We need occasionally to leave them undirected, in order that we may receive these messages by wireless from the Unknown. We need to have the instrument working at its greatest perfection, be undirected and receptive.

I am not advocating a mystic ideal. This imagery is fruitful, whether these ideas and ideals come wholly from within and are the adjustment and readjustment even of material products, or whether they come to us as the response of the individual to external stimuli.

The fundamental characteristic of youth is growth—happy, continuous growth. Is not the reason why so many of us look back to youth as the period of greatest happiness because it was the time of greatest growth ? I think that the people whom I know as most happy in middle and advanced years are those persons who have kept on growing.

The as yet relatively httle known researches of Cajal and Flechsig have shown us that the tangential fibres of the brain may continue their growth at least through middle life, and it appears also that the fibres are in some way directly related to intelligence.

Most people seem to stop growing soon after they become twenty. Other people keep on growing for varying periods. The duration of life's growth is governed partly by heredity and it is partly under our own control. It is limited by forced work without rest and margin. It is promoted by wholesome living. It is interfered with by routine work without a break. We must retain the habit of doing unhabitual things if we are to grow.

All this may seem like the statement of an impossible ideal. It is not. There will come weeks and months when every ounce of strength and every moment of time must be spent on the accomplishment of certain things. But when this is a man's constant life, when it occurs month after month and year after year, then it indicates that th^

work has mastered the man. The man is no longer the master; he is the slave. It means that his growth and his capacity to do larger and larger things are prevented.

I know men as secretaries of Young Men's Christian Associations, as college physical directors, as the owners or directors of immense corporations; I know women as housewives and mothers of large families, who have preserved this balance between work and rest, so that they have continued growing, so that their ideals have enlarged from decade to decade, so that their response to life has been ever larger.

But with these people there has been a clear conprehension of the tremendous tendency of the time away from margin, away from rest, away from balance. They have set their faces like a flint and have not allowed the immediate pressure of the moment, the drag of the deadly detail, to so chain them down as to prevent their moving toward the far larger and more important ideal that is farther in the distance.

A dime held close enough to the eye will hut out the whole world. The small duty

close at hand may shut out all vision, all ideals. The great ideals are never near. The small duty is always with us. There are always things to be done. In order to achieve the greatest which is within each one of us, we must balance between the small duties which could never be completely done—had we ten times our present time and strength—and the distant ideals. We must be able to say to the immediate and small, Stand back! That is your place! This is the time for rest, for margin, for assimilation, for growth."

Rest is as important as work. Dreams must precede action. Concentrated art is not art, and the acquiring of facts is not growth.

THE END

Lightning Source UK Ltd.
Milton Keynes UK
UKHW031933090220
358432UK00007B/158